JUST ONCE

But looking down into Lady Cassandra's face, Ben very much wished he could do as he pleased. And he wished, devoutly, that he could kiss the Incomparable Cassandra. Just once. Just so he would truly know what he had missed. That would be foolish beyond belief. But, for once in his life, could he do the *wrong* thing?

"Ben?" Lady Cassandra's eyes were concerned. "Are you all right?"

No, he thought. *I am not all right. I am very, very wrong. But this may be the last chance I have in life to throw caution to the wind.*

The Incomparable Cassandra

Laura Paquet

ZEBRA BOOKS
Kensington Publishing Corp.
www.kensingtonbooks.com

CHAPTER ONE

"Good heavens!" Lady Elinor Blythe laid the letter she had been reading on the polished mahogany breakfast table and rubbed her eyes. "Ben left Dorsetshire three days ago. He expects to arrive in London any day now—possibly tonight, if the weather has been favorable."

"Tonight?" Lady Cassandra Blythe turned from the sideboard, crossed the room, and set her plate on the table. She regarded her sister-in-law's pale face. "But you did not expect him until next week at the earliest."

Elinor shook her head. "He seems to have left home almost immediately after sending his letter accepting my invitation. I had forgotten how decisive Ben could be. Funny, when we were children, I knew him so well. But the years go by, and one forgets."

Cassandra noted the regret that seemed to seep into her sister-in-law's voice whenever she spoke of her estranged brother. Truly, it was unfortunate that Elinor and her twin had not seen each other for ten years. But as far as Cassandra could tell, the fault lay entirely with Benjamin Rowland, the Earl of Winchfield. If he hadn't been so high in the instep, he would have made amends with his sister years ago.

Elinor, after all, had extended a series of olive branches.

"You are well prepared for his visit," Cassandra assured Elinor. "His rooms have been aired ever since he wrote his initial reply, and the linens are all ready."

"Yes, but *I'm* not quite ready," Elinor said with a short laugh. "And I have not yet checked with Cook to see if she has located my mother's gingersnap recipe. Ben loves gingersnaps." She stood, leaving most of her breakfast uneaten. "And I must tell Alice and David that their uncle may arrive this very day. They have been beside themselves with curiosity about him, and I promised them that I would inform them the moment I knew when he was to arrive." Elinor placed her napkin beside her plate and crossed the room.

"Is there anything I can do to help with the preparations?" Cassandra asked.

Elinor turned from the door and gave her a pleading look. "Just be welcoming. I know you think he has mistreated Richard and me, but truly, he was only acting as he thought best. I have forgiven him, and I wish with all my heart that you and Richard could find it in your hearts to forgive him, too."

Cassandra smiled what she hoped was an encouraging smile. "I shall do my best for your sake, my dear. Although I *do* think you have been very ill-used."

"That is all in the past. If things are to be mended, 'tis I who must mend them. Ben is far too proud to admit that he might have been wrong."

Cassandra snorted. "No one is right all the time, and if he thinks—"

"Please don't."

The whispered plea stopped Cassandra in midsentence. She realized that her sister-in-law was much more intent on building new bridges than Cassandra had thought. And if that was the way Elinor wanted to approach the situation, the least Cassandra could do was support her. After all, Elinor was her dearest friend in the world, and rarely asked for much.

"I am sorry, Ellie. I promise you, I shall be the soul of welcome when your brother arrives."

Elinor's smile was wide and grateful. "Thank you. I knew you would be. It is just so important that he have a good visit in London. And remember, if you can think of any plain, placid ladies—"

"I'll be certain to let you know."

Elinor closed the door behind her and Cassandra returned her attention to her tea and toast.

That last request, somehow, bothered Cassandra more than all the other worries and demands that seemed to be piling up in advance of the earl's visit. Lord Winchfield had apparently deigned to visit his sister solely because he needed help finding a quiet, biddable, malleable wife.

Just like most of the other gentlemen in London, Cassandra thought as she smeared her toast with strawberry preserves. Those who didn't want an exotic hothouse flower to escort to society functions like a prize racehorse wanted a homespun, simpering miss who would be so grateful for their attention that she would never dream of looking at another male.

Cassandra had no trouble attracting the former type of gentleman, she reflected as she chewed on her sticky toast. The fates had been kind to her in the matter of face and figure, and she had already enjoyed several Seasons as something of a *ton* belle. But most of the gentlemen who pursued her were disappointed to realize that under that crown of gold hair a human brain with desires and thoughts of its own actually resided.

She sighed. Thank heaven for Perry—Mr. Russell, rather, as she had to remember to call him when they were out in society. Peregrine Russell was the one man in the world, aside from her brother, who seemed to appreciate her mind as well as the picture she presented in an elegant ball gown. It was too bad, really, that it seemed he had little interest in becoming anything more than her friend. But at least he was a most amusing person to talk to at parties, and he gave her excellent comments on her work.

With a set of tiny silver tongs, she extracted a cube of sugar from a blue Wedgwood bowl and dropped it into her cup, which she then filled with steaming tea from a matching pot. She inhaled the rich fragrance as she stirred the brew.

It was unlikely that Lord Winchfield would be the least bit amusing, Cassandra thought as she raised the cup to her lips. From what Elinor had told her over the years, she had conjured up a picture rather akin to an illustration of the Angel of Death she had once seen in a religious tract.

Surely he couldn't be that bad, she thought as she sipped her tea. Just because he had overreacted to Elinor and Richard's elopement did not mean he was entirely devoid of good qualities.

But neither did it mean that he would be a pleasant person to be around, she thought. She spared a moment's gratitude for the fact that Richard and Elinor lived in Blythe House, one of the largest mansions in Mayfair. It shouldn't be too difficult to stay far away from the imposing Earl of Winchfield when he arrived.

Cassandra had promised Elinor she would be cordial to her brother. That did not mean she had to spend any more time in the man's company than was absolutely necessary.

Benjamin Rowland, the Earl of Winchfield, tugged in frustration at his neckcloth and finally succeeded in twisting open the last knot. The fabric now hung around his neck in a limp, damp strand.

He applied himself to the task of retying it in a tidy fashion. The knot Tyson had created earlier had been a huge, windblown-looking thing that hadn't suited Ben at all.

It was not a simple endeavor. Five minutes later, he had created some semblance of a Mathematical knot, although he suspected it was a rather poor version. He rarely wore a neckcloth around the estate; it served only to inhibit him when he was pursuing his studies, as it had an unfortunate tendency to come undone and tumble into the anthills. Were it not for church services, meetings with his estate manager, and the local assemblies, he would never don one of the demmed things at all.

He glanced at his reflection in the mirror again and sighed. The neckcloth looked more like a scullery maid's scrubbing rag than something a gentleman would wear.

"Tyson!" he called out. "I need some assistance!"

Instantly, his towheaded valet appeared at the door of the small room. "Yes, m'lord?" Tyson's eyes shifted to his employer's throat, and Ben thought he detected a faint expression of annoyance flit across the servant's face. It disappeared almost immediately, to be replaced by a bland, impassive look.

"I seem to have made a disaster of my neckcloth," Ben muttered.

"I wouldn't say a 'disaster,' m'lord."

"Whatever you would call it, can you fix it?"

The valet reached out to finger the limp cravat. "I'm not certain. There's little starch left." He eyed his employer's hair. "If I may ask, were you displeased with your coiffure?"

Ben shifted his gaze to the mirror once more. "It seemed a bit messy, Tyson. I merely straightened it." He hadn't given a second thought to his hair, so consumed had he been by worries about his neckcloth.

What an immense amount of time one could consume fussing about one's appearance. But for once in his life, he actually cared how he looked. If Tyson was right, they would arrive at Elinor's house by late afternoon, and he wanted to make a good impression on his sister. She had been living in the bosom of the *haute ton* for a decade now. The last thing he wanted to appear as was the eccentric country squire—although, secretly, he suspected that was exactly what he was.

"The hair is supposed to look rather disheveled," Tyson said with a very slight edge of irritation. "Such a style is all the go these days. It is called à la Titus."

Ben raised his eyebrows. "And how have you come to be such an expert on London fashions? You have ventured no further from Dorsetshire than I have these last ten years."

Tyson's round face was mulish. "I read, m'lord, and make an effort to keep up. 'Tisn't difficult, if one applies oneself."

And if one doesn't spend one's days lost in contemplation of the tiny, fascinating world of bugs, Ben added silently.

He *was* somewhat isolated, Ben realized with a start. He kept up with news of politics and had a basic grasp of the world of sport, but aside from those two topics he had no more notion of what went on beyond the borders of his estate than he had of advanced mathematics or ancient philosophy. He had left his studies at Oxford young, to return to Dorsetshire and assume the duties of the estate. As a result, he had long felt that he did not know the basic things that many other gentlemen his age took for granted.

"Yes, well, Tyson, I apologize for not trusting your judgment," he said. "Have the trunks been loaded onto the carriage?"

"Yes, m'lord. I just shifted the last one into place m'self."

"Then I suppose it is too late to repair the damage I have done. I expect your tools and all the fresh neckcloths have been packed."

Tyson grinned, crossed the room, and pulled open a small drawer in the bureau. He extracted a single crisp neckcloth and a small hairbrush.

"Why were these not packed, Tyson?"

"I had a strange feeling we might be needing 'em, m'lord."

Ben grinned despite himself. "I suppose I can be a bit willful."

"'Tisn't my place to say." Tyson motioned his employer into a chair. "I will try to revive your hair first, and then I shall retie your neckcloth. By the way, how did you flatten out the curls? Your head looks as though it has been slicked with glue."

"A great deal of pomade."

The valet grimaced. "Please, m'lord. The rage these days is for very natural-looking hair. Lord Byron and his ilk have convinced everyone that we must all live as wild children."

"I am sorry I doubted you. If you wish to color it purple, I promise I shall not complain." An unfamiliar pang of self-doubt stabbed him, and he felt cold dots of sweat beading his forehead. What if he arrived in London and Elinor laughed at him? What if instead of reconciliation, he found only scorn?

He sighed. It might have been a decade since he and Elinor had set eyes on each other, but the breach had not been absolute. They still wrote letters to each other monthly, and although he did not know her as well as he had when they were children, he thought he still sensed how Elinor would react. She had a soft heart, and he doubted she would turn him away, although she would have every right to do so. He had sustained their coolness for far too long.

"I don't think purple hair will be necessary," Tyson, remarked as he rubbed Benjamin's coiffure with a rough towel. "It would make you rather conspicuous in the ballrooms of Mayfair."

Ballrooms. Ben repressed a shudder. "The last thing I want to do is be conspicuous." To be honest, the *last* thing he wanted to do was go within a hundred miles of a ballroom. But it had come time to marry, and it seemed that Mayfair ballrooms were the place where England's marriageable chits were to be found.

They certainly weren't to be found in Dorsetshire. Heaven knows, he'd tried.

He'd begun searching several years ago, by attending the dances held in the assembly rooms in Winchfield village. Women had been willing enough to accept his invitations to dance. A title and a comfortable country estate lent remarkable luster to one's charms.

In the small mirror, he watched Tyson with suspicion as the valet removed the last traces of pomade, then attacked his employer's hair with a fresh towel dipped in water from the ewer.

"I'd have suggested a bath, my lord, but I didn't want to delay our departure any longer than necessary."

Ben nodded. "You were right—I want to reach London by nightfall, at the latest. Proceed."

As Tyson continued to maul his locks, Ben's thoughts drifted back to his wife-hunting efforts in Dorsetshire. The whole enterprise had been a disaster. The fact that he had had to limit his search to women of a certain station had hampered him to some degree. It wouldn't do for the Earl of Winchfield to marry someone common. After all, he had to do his part to repair the damage to the family name done by Elinor's elopement.

So many of the women who came to the assembly rooms were outside the sphere of his interest by pure accident of birth. The rest—well, the rest had been an uninspiring lot. Except for Georgina Wells, of course. But he refused to think about her.

After their most unfortunate association, he had decided—quite logically—that lively women just created trouble in their wake. It seemed much more prudent, for him and for the reputation of the estate, to concentrate his efforts on finding a quiet, proper mistress for Winchfield Hall. But that was easier said than done.

He had had high hopes for Lady Mary Soles, because her mama had explained that Lady Mary's primary virtue was her quiet nature. But *quiet*, in Lady Mary's case, had meant that she was terrified of just about everything, from riding to unfamiliar foods. Her phobias extended, unfortunately, to insects. When he had told her of his research with ants, the color had drained from her face and she had begged off their dance in order to sit down with her fan and a glass of lemonade.

All the women he met, to his frustration, seemed to fall into one of two patterns: timid as mice, like Mary, or boisterous as rabbits, like Georgina. All he wanted was—well, what did he want? He struggled to think of a metaphor, wincing as Tyson tugged a bit too forcefully at one dark curl.

"Sorry, m'lord."

" 'Tis no matter." What sort of animal would his ideal wife most closely resemble? He pondered the question for a moment or two until the perfect image struck him. The woman he sought would be like a cat by a fireside: sleek, serene, and self-contained. Someone who would neither need nor desire much attention from him, yet would be a calming influence in his home. Someone who would raise decorous children who would be a credit to him and to the estate.

Yes, that was it. He needed a human mother cat. But did such a creature exist, even in London?

He devoutly hoped so. Already, he had wasted far too much time on this project. With luck, he would be able to find a likely prospect within a week or two, to avoid imposing on Elinor's hospitality for too long.

Elinor. He sighed as Tyson disheveled his hair once more. Even if Ben didn't succeed in finding a wife on this trip, it would be good if he could repair the rift between himself and his sister—a rift that had been largely of his making, he acknowledged. Yes, Elinor had been headstrong to run off with Richard Blythe. Her behavior had reflected poorly on the family. But that had all happened years ago, and he had to admit—grudgingly—that he might have been wrong to oppose the match. Elinor's letters, to his immense relief, seemed to be those of a woman most content with the way her life had progressed. She referred often, with fondness, to Richard and the children— the latter amorphous beings in whom Ben could not quite believe, since he had never set eyes on them. Perhaps she was lying about her happiness, but Ben didn't think so. He might not have seen his sister in a decade, but twins had an instinctive understanding of each other that no amount of time and animosity could dissipate.

Tyson laid down his bush.

"I believe this is the best we can hope for," the valet said, eyeing the coiffure—if one could call the rat's nest on Ben's pate by such a grand name. "I hope for better luck with the neckcloth."

"Thank you for your assistance."

As Tyson shook out the linen cloth, Ben reined in his fears about the reception he would receive from Elinor. If she was still angry with him, that was her affair.

CHAPTER TWO

The house certainly *looked* respectable, Ben thought as he let the shiny brass knocker fall against the door.

The door was pulled open immediately. To his shock, it was not a butler who stood on the threshold, but his sister herself. He might not have seen her for a decade, but her unruly mass of dark curls—so like his own—left little doubt that the grinning woman who faced him was Elinor.

"Ben!" she cried, hurling herself at him with such force that he almost tumbled backward down the shallow front stairs. Even Tyson, who had just reached the stoop with an armload of luggage, took a cautious step back.

"Ellie." He wrapped his arms around her and squeezed tight, burying his suddenly warm face in her hair. He hadn't realized, until this moment, how much he had missed his twin. It was demmed good to see her again.

They embraced silently for a moment or two, until he realized the spectacle they presented. "Is this the way you greet everyone who comes to your door?" he asked, setting her firmly away from him but smiling to take the sting from the action.

"Of course!" she said, standing aside and motioning

him into the foyer. "It takes the costermongers by surprise, but they've become used to it."

He frowned as he stepped into the house. "But don't the costermongers come to the kitchen entrance, rather than the front door?"

Ellie laughed. "Certainly! You haven't been rusticating so long in Dorsetshire that you've forgotten how to recognize a joke, have you?"

Perhaps he had. "No," he said, feeling every inch the country fool. "I'm just a bit tired from the journey, and not thinking—"

"Oh, don't apologize. I shouldn't have teased you the moment you arrived." She watched as Tyson set down a large portmanteau and exited again. "Have you much baggage?"

Was she trying to determine how long he intended to stay? "Enough, I suppose. It seems like a gargantuan amount, actually. Tyson insisted on bringing just about every article of clothing I owned, including some odd garments he insisted I have made up by a tailor in Dorchester last fall." He remembered, with trepidation, the skintight pantaloons that extended down to his ankles and then strapped under his feet. He thought they looked ridiculous, and had told Tyson so at the time. Even though he had later seen Viscount Ashmorland wearing a very similar ensemble in the Winchfield assembly rooms, he still wondered whether that had not been an anomaly.

"I'm glad to hear it, because I have quite the array of social engagements arranged for you," she said, leading him across the sunny foyer and up a curving staircase. "Everyone is waiting for you in the drawing room."

"Everyone?" Surely she hadn't taken his request

too much to heart and arranged to have a series of London belles here to meet him, before he'd even had a chance to wash away the grime of his journey? And what had she meant by an "array of social engagements"?

To his immense disgust, his stomach had begun to roil as it once had when he'd spent days aboard a stuffy ship on a trip to Bristol.

"No one intimidating, I assure you. Just Richard and Cassandra."

Cassandra? He wracked his brain to place the name and then remembered that she was Blythe's younger sister, who was spending the Season with them in London, as usual. If he recalled Elinor's letters correctly, this Cassandra sounded like a most intimidating creature, always dressed in the latest stare of fashion and fighting off the attentions of any number of beaux. Even though he cared not a whit what any member of the Blythe family thought of him, he couldn't help but glance down at his dusty boots with dismay.

"Oh, don't worry about your clothes," Elinor said, reading his mind as she always had, as if they had just seen each other only yesterday. "You'll have plenty of time to refresh yourself before dinner. But we have all been anticipating your arrival so eagerly that I wanted to introduce you as soon as you arrived, if I could. I hope you don't mind?"

He did, but it would be churlish to say so. Elinor's excitement was so genuine—and such a relief, given his fears that she would be displeased to see him— that he couldn't refuse her request.

"I would be pleased to meet them. Are the children here as well?"

"Sadly, no—they will be so disappointed to have

missed your arrival. But they were so full of high spirits that I asked their nurse to take them to the park so that they could expend some of that excess energy. I expect they shall return within the hour."

They had reached a pair of white paneled doors guarded by a footman. The servant bowed, then threw open the doors with a flourish.

Ben felt rather as though he were an actor making his grand entrance into some monumental production. At least, he thought his sweaty palms and thundering heart were akin to those an actor might experience on opening night. Having never met a thespian, or even seen a play, he couldn't be sure.

"Richard, you remember Ben?" Elinor asked as she preceded him into the room.

Ben doubted that his brother-in-law would have forgotten him. The last time they had met, Ben had come within a hairsbreadth of challenging Lord Richard Blythe to a duel.

"Of course I remember your brother," said a tall gentleman, rising from his seat at a baize-covered card table and extending his hand. "Winchfield."

Blythe had gained some weight over the last few years, looking less the unformed youth than he once had, but was otherwise almost unchanged. It was hard to believe that it had been a decade since they had exchanged such heated words at Winchfield Hall.

Had the years been as kind to Ben himself? Impossible to say. He had no one but servants around to offer their opinion on such matters and they, of course, rarely did so.

"Blythe." Ben reached out and shook the hand of the man he had once blamed for souring his family's hopes.

Blythe gave him a brief, chilly smile. Obviously,

Elinor had primed her husband to be polite. The least Ben could do was respond in kind.

"Thank you for having me as your guest," he said. "Your home is lovely, and it will be good to stay in such charming surroundings on my first visit to London."

Blythe chuckled. "The charm of the surroundings is due solely to the skills of your sister and mine. They are the experts on matters of home management, not I. Speaking of which, please allow me to present my sister, Lady Cassandra Blythe." He nodded toward the other side of the table, and a young woman stood. As she walked toward him, Ben realized that he truly had spent too many years focusing on little but ants, not to have noticed Lady Cassandra the moment he walked into the room.

Like her brother, Lady Cassandra was fair and tall. But while Blythe seemed slightly ill at ease with his height, she carried hers like a queen. As she crossed the room toward him, she almost seemed to glide.

Her cream-colored day dress was more elaborate than many gowns he had seen women wear at the evening assemblies in Winchfield. The hem sported layers of ruffles edged with lace and blue ribbons, and the sleeves were puffed up like enormous mushrooms. A wide blue ribbon encircled the gown and trailed behind her like streamers on a kite. But even the layers of fabric, ribbon, and lace could not conceal some very appealing curves.

She held out her hand and curtsied, and he was happy to hide his face—and hopefully, his thoughts—with a deep bow. Thank goodness she could not read his mind, as Elinor could.

"I am pleased to make your acquaintance, Lord Winchfield." Despite her proper words, she looked anything but delighted. Her brother had at least tried to smile. As soon as was polite, she extracted her hand from his and returned to her chair.

"I see you were in the midst of a card game when I arrived," he said, sitting down on a low, Egyptian-style divan. "Do not let me interrupt you."

"It is of no import. We were just whiling away the time until you arrived," Elinor said as she sat at the opposite end of the divan and picked up a small silver bell. "I'll just ring for tea."

"Yes, it is no matter to put aside our game," her sister-in-law added in a loud voice. "Here in London, we do little that is so vital that it cannot be interrupted."

Ben did not miss the quelling look his sister shot Lady Cassandra. It was evident that he had not mistaken Blythe's sister's ill will toward him. Inwardly, he bristled. Who was she that she felt she could judge him?

No sooner had his outrage bubbled up than it ebbed away. She had every right to condemn him. After all, it was solely due to his stubbornness that he and Elinor had remained estranged for so long. Granted, Elinor had created the rift by eloping. But he had nursed his grudge far longer than was seemly, and that foolish behavior was all Lady Cassandra knew of him.

Not that it mattered. Within a week or two, if he was lucky, he would find a suitable female, make an offer, and be back in Dorsetshire before the ducklings on his pond were fully fledged. While ants were his specialty, he enjoyed studying all the creatures on his estate, and he had started a particularly fruitful inquiry into the habits of ducks the preceding summer. It would be good to update that research while the ducklings were still young.

"Lord Winchfield?"

Damn. He hated being caught woolgathering, although he supposed he should be used to it by now. It happened often enough at the village assemblies, when he would find himself fading away as the ladies descended into a detailed dissection of the latest social news.

"Yes, Lady Cassandra?"

"I asked if you had had a good journey."

"Yes, quite, thank you. It progressed quite quickly, as the weather was clement and the roads in good repair. I found it much less tiring than I anticipated it would be."

She nodded. "So you will be well refreshed for the rout on Friday."

He looked at Elinor. "Rout?"

His sister smiled. "We've organized a bit of a party in honor of your arrival. Ever since you wrote that you would be coming to visit, I've been sending out invitations to every likely young lady I know."

"And she knows quite a few," Lady Cassandra interjected with a chuckle.

"Many have already replied and said they would be delighted to come," Elinor continued. "I'm expecting a crowd."

A crowd? On Friday—three days hence? Once again, he felt his stomach churning. And once again, he cursed himself for being so fainthearted about this whole affair. He'd been managing an estate of more than twelve hundred acres since the age of nineteen— at first with the nominal help of a guardian, but for nine years with no assistance. Surely managing a roomful of marriage-minded misses would be child's play in comparison?

He smiled. "Thank you, Ellie, for going to so much trouble."

She laughed. He'd forgotten how much he missed that lovely peal. "I don't need much prodding to arrange a social event. And since I've been dangling a rich, reclusive earl as a carrot, it's astonishing how quick every Incomparable in London has been to respond to my invitation."

"Incomparables? I appreciate the thought, Ellie, but I don't think—"

"Don't worry. I've also invited scores of less-intimidating ladies." She paused, tapping her fingers against the marble top of the table at her side. "Let me see. Well, there's Miss Seaforth, for example."

"Oh yes!" Lady Cassandra exclaimed. "Miss Seaforth would not terrify a fly."

Was she having fun at his expense? He glared at her, but her countenance remained as innocent as a child's, except for a slight gleam in her wide blue eyes.

"And then there's Lady Susan Phipps," Lady Cassandra added. "It is widely known that she has never voiced an independent thought. I'm surprised she has not become the belle of the Marriage Mart already." There was no mistaking that mischievous gleam in her eye now. She was most definitely mocking him.

Well, he would not rise to the bait. If he could but remain polite and unmoved by her barbs, perhaps she would realize that he was, indeed, a country bore, and move on to more enticing game.

"I am eager to meet all the ladies you have invited," he said, ignoring Lady Cassandra and returning his attention to his sister. And, in truth, he was eager, in a way. Eager to get through this rout, and any other social functions he'd be obliged to attend, so that he could conclude this business.

There was no doubt that he had to marry. His father's family was not notably robust, and he was the sole heir to the title. If he died without issue, the earldom would die with him, and he refused to even countenance that possibility.

But he had never dreamed that it would be so difficult to find a biddable wife who did not bore him to tears. But perhaps boredom wasn't the worst fate in the world, he thought, remembering Georgina Wells. She had not been boring, but she had been far from biddable.

He fingered the ring in his pocket. It had been his mother's betrothal ring, and he'd been loath to pack it in a traveling case where the small circlet of rubies might get misplaced, or even pilfered at a wayside inn. He'd kept it in his pocket throughout the trip as a reminder of his purpose in London. Unfortunately, whenever he touched it, he was also reminded of the night he'd planned to give it to Georgina. Thank heaven he'd discovered her perfidy before he'd made his offer.

He closed his hand around the ring. If he avoided bright, beautiful women like Georgina, he should be able to succeed in his marriage quest with his dignity intact.

Lord Winchfield, Lady Cassandra decided conclusively later that evening as she made ready for bed, was a pompous bore. Not once had he even smiled at any of the little jokes she and Elinor had traded over dinner, nor at the amusing stories Richard had told later in the evening over cards.

Not that that excused her poor treatment of the earl, she thought as she laid her dress on the velvet-upholstered chair next to the wardrobe. She grimaced. Elinor had asked her to be kind to the earl, and Cassandra had been cutting. It was no way to repay her sister-in-law, who had been such a good friend over the years.

Elinor was determined to help her brother find a wife. Perhaps Cassandra could help on that score. Surely she knew some bookish female who might suit the earl?

Cassandra wracked her brains as she picked up the nightrail Agnes had left at the foot of the bed. Most of her friends were bubbly and outgoing. She had never had much patience for milk-and-water misses.

As she wriggled into the soft silk nightdress, she remembered Anne Lewis, the daughter of friends of her parents. The last time Cassandra had visited the senior Blythes in Lincolnshire, her mother had urged her to be kind to the young woman.

"She hasn't a spark of originality to her, but she's really very sweet and extremely shy," the marchioness had said with a smile. "I know it would mean so much to Dorothea and Andrew if you would invite her to visit every so often, and make a point of speaking to her at social functions."

The latter had not been an issue, since Anne Lewis avoided large parties. But Cassandra had asked her to tea several times, and had arranged a small excursion to Astley's Circus. The pale, freckled girl had been grateful for the courtesy, and Cassandra had felt slightly shamefaced at her reluctance to do even that much.

She hadn't seen Miss Lewis in almost two weeks. Perhaps she could arrange to have her come to call while Lord Winchfield was home?

No, that would be far too obvious and Miss Lewis would flee like a frightened kitten. It had to look accidental. She would put her mind to the problem. Perhaps a "chance" meeting in Hyde Park would do the trick?

Satisfied that she had made at least a little progress toward fulfilling her promise to Elinor, she pulled on the nightrail's matching robe and moved toward the spacious dressing table.

Tomorrow, she vowed, she would be more pleasant to Lord Winchfield. It cost her nothing but a bit of integrity to pretend that she thought the earl a paragon. And he would be gone soon enough, all being well. Although he lacked a great deal in personality, in Cassandra's opinion, it was almost certain that there would be a number of misses in London willing to overlook that fact for the chance to become a countess and mistress of one of the finest estates in Dorsetshire.

The surprise was that the earl hadn't been able to find such a miss out in the country. Perhaps he was just too selective.

She sat down with a thump on the pretty little chair in front of her dressing table. Lord Winchfield was handsome enough, she supposed, that he could afford to be choosy.

Cassandra had been surprised upon meeting him to discover that he cut a most appealing figure. Perhaps due to her earlier vision of him as the devil incarnate, or to the fact that he'd spent a decade rusticating in Dorsetshire, she'd pictured him as short, bland, and pasty. It had come as something of a shock to discover that he was taller even than her brother, with wild dark curls that looked as though they had resisted a determined effort to tame them. When he had fixed her with that stare, his hazel eyes had snapped with annoyance. Yet rather than abashed, she had found herself intrigued.

Good heavens, she thought as she took the lid off the enameled box she used to store her hairpins. What could possibly be appealing about such a high-in-the-instep country cousin? He was so beyond the pale of the types of gentlemen with whom she usually kept company as to be almost another species altogether.

It had something to do with the way he carried himself, she decided. Unlike Richard, who always seemed slightly embarrassed by his height, Lord Winchfield walked and moved as one completely comfortable in his own skin.

Be that as it may, he was still a stuffed shirt, she thought as she began to pull out the pins that supported her elaborate coiffure. The process of taking down her hair was always somewhat arduous, which was why she preferred to change into her nightclothes before beginning it. By the time her hair was brushed out and plaited for the night, she was usually more than ready for sleep.

As if cued by a stage manager, Agnes scratched at the door and then opened it at Cassandra's reply. "Ready for my assistance, m'lady?"

"Yes, please." Cassandra put down the pin she was holding and twisted about so that her maid could easily take down the rest of her hair.

"It seems a bit tangled," Agnes remarked as she continued the task Cassandra had started.

"I went for a walk in Hyde Park this afternoon, after Lord Winchfield's arrival, and the wind had picked up. I tried to straighten my hair before dinner, but I suspect I did not do a perfect job."

Agnes nodded, unable to speak for the moment around a mouthful of pins. When she had extracted them and placed them in the box on the dressing table, she asked, "So what do you think of Lord Winchfield, then?"

Cassandra hesitated. It was forward of Agnes to ask such a question, but understandable. The older woman had served at Winchfield Hall for many years before accompanying Elinor during her elopement a decade before. She had known the twin siblings since the day they were born.

Cassandra suspected that the maid would not take kindly to any suggestion that her former employer—of whom she always spoke in the most respectful tones—was anything less than admirable.

"It is good to see him reunited with Lady Elinor," she said finally.

"Aye, that it is," Agnes replied, pulling out another cluster of pins. A long blond curl fell down Cassandra's back. "Those two were once as thick as thieves, I can tell you. It seemed unnatural, so it did, for them to go for so long without setting eyes on each other."

"What were they like, as children?"

Agnes tossed more pins into the enameled box. "You rarely saw one without the other, till young Lord Ben—I'm sorry, Lord Winchfield—went away to Oxford. He even prevailed upon their parents not to send him to Eton, but instead to let him and Elinor be schooled at home by masters, so that they should not be separated." The maid picked up a silver-backed brush and began to pull the knots from Cassandra's hair. "Perhaps if their parents had had more children, there would not have been such a strong bond between the twins. As it was, they had only each other."

This part of the story Cassandra knew. The twins' birth had greatly weakened their mother, who remained a semi-invalid until she passed away when Elinor and her brother were fourteen. It had been evident early that there would be no more children.

A silence fell between Cassandra and the maid for a few moments. Then, as Agnes shifted the candlestick on the dressing table in order to shed better light on her work, she sighed.

"What is it, Agnes?"

The maid looked uneasy. "I've always felt a mite bad for runnin' out on Lord Winchfield. Young gentleman that he was, with so much to handle at such a tender age, and no help forthcomin' from Lord Tanner."

"Their guardian? The one who had the stroke?"

"Aye. He had little choice but to leave the twins to their own devices." She paused briefly as she worked a knot free. "And for Lord Winchfield to be on poor terms with his sister into the bargain couldn't have been easy. But Lady Elinor implored me to come with her, and I could hardly let her catch the mail coach alone, could I? For that's what she would have done."

Cassandra had never once given a thought to what it must have been like for the earl to be left alone to manage his estate at the age of twenty, only a year after his father's death. She had assumed that such a fate wouldn't trouble the devil incarnate one bit. Suddenly, she had a picture of the earl—likely less broad in the shoulders and less confident of mien—looking out his front door to realize that he was indeed alone with his vast responsibilities. Perhaps that was why he had been so reluctant to see Elinor married to a man who planned to take her far away.

It was none of her affair, Cassandra told herself. He was a man in possession of both great wealth and good health, with no impediments to travel. If he had been lonely, he could have easily come to London to visit his sister years ago.

"I just never thought it would be ten years before I'd see the young earl again," the maid continued as she finished brushing Cassandra's hair and laid the heavy brush back on the table. "One long plait tonight, m'lady? Or would you prefer two?"

"One is fine, thank you, Agnes." To her astonishment— it had been a day for surprises, really—she found herself with more than a passing curiosity to learn more about Elinor's boorish brother. And there was no one, aside from Ellie herself, better to ask than Agnes. "Was Lord Winchfield always so stuffy?"

The maid smiled as she split Cassandra's long hair into three thick tails. "I wouldn't describe him as stuffy, m'lady. Standoffish, perhaps. Reserved. He was never the social creature that Lady Elinor is. She lived for supper parties and dances and picnics. He would go with her, but he would often grumble that he had other things he'd rather do. Even then, he was much more content in the barn, poking at some little animal and making sketches, than he ever was at some fancy party. But he would go, to please his sister, and I think 'twas good for him. I've often wondered how he's done, all these years, with no one to encourage him to be social."

"He doesn't look like the sort of man who spends all day in the barn, hunched over some study."

Agnes tilted her head sideways in an unspoken question.

"It's just," Cassandra stammered, "that he is so tanned. And he looks . . . fit. As though he spends a lot of time outdoors." Why were her cheeks suddenly warm? Surely these facts were apparent to anyone who looked at the gentleman?

If Agnes noticed her strange manner, she chose not to comment on it. Focusing on the hair she was twisting, she said. "It's a large estate, and he must needs be riding around it a lot to keep things in order. My sister still works there, and she sends me the odd note. Thank God the nuns back home taught us to read and write."

Cassandra nodded, well used to the maid's digressions.

"Anyway, our Maisie says the earl's a great one for checking in with the tenants, making sure there are no fences that need mending nor roofs in poor repair. He does many of the repairs himself, or else he makes sure there are others assigned to do it, before haring back to the barn and his animals." She came to the end of the plait and reached across the dressing table for a ribbon. Once she had secured her work, she looked up. "Will there be anything else tonight?"

"No, thank you, Agnes."

When the maid had left, closing the door softly behind her, Cassandra picked up the candle, crossed the room, discarded her robe, and climbed into the high, old-fashioned bed. Pulling the lavender-scented sheets up to her chin, she leaned over and blew out the candle, then settled against the thick pillows.

Usually, she had no trouble drifting into unconsciousness, but this evening sleep refused to come. What had she been thinking, asking all those questions? By morning, the news would likely have spread throughout the household staff that Lady Cassandra had a most *unusual* interest in the mistress's brother. Agnes was a dear, but she was the most notorious gossip in Blythe House.

Botheration. Cassandra sat up, fluffed up her pillow, and sank back into it.

What did she care what the servants thought? It wasn't as though she wasn't already a daily source of entertainment to them.

She knew that the two parlor maids, Tilly and Bette, thought her a glamorous creature. "Look, she has *another* gent come to call!" she'd heard one whisper in awed tones to the other as she'd descended the stairs one afternoon. "That makes five today alone! And all of them sending flowers!"

That had been a chaotic week. Last year, at the beginning of the Season, Cassandra had made quite an impression at the Duke of Canford's annual spring ball. A number of gentlemen newly arrived in Town had vied for her favors, jostling each other to reap the prize of a dance. At the end of the Season, they had shared some laughter about the foolishness of it all.

Cassandra enjoyed fun—probably more than anyone else she knew. Perhaps that's why the men who were drawn to her seemed interested in nothing else. For a few years, the rounds of parties and balls, the *on-dits* and the competition to come up with the best witty remark at the theater had been diverting. But Cassandra was four-and-twenty now, and the appeal of such youthful interests had begun to pale for her.

For the gentlemen in her circle, however, there was

little more diverting in life than talk of the latest scandal, the best tailor, the fastest horse at Newmarket, or the latest faux pas committed at the most stylish parties. Whenever she tried to turn the talk to anything else, she would be met with blank stares.

Perhaps that's why the boring Lord Winchfield had caught her interest. Say what one might about him, it would be impossible to classify him as a foppish fribble.

She sighed. Again, her thoughts had returned to the prickly earl. What was it about him, she wondered.

Then, all of a sudden, she knew.

Scrambling out of bed, she felt her way along the familiar perimeter of the room until she reached the mantelpiece. Within moments, she had lit the brace of candles kept there for just such an occasion.

She brought the candlestick to her desk and set it down. After pulling on her robe, she returned to the desk, riffled through some papers and extracted the one she wanted. It was the second scene of the second act, and she suddenly had a very good idea for fixing it.

Since starting work on the play two months ago, she'd been having trouble making one of the characters believable. Every line she wrote for Sir Humphrey Mills seemed flat and trite. He was supposed to be a pompous prig, a foil for the wittier characters. But the problem was she didn't keep company with many stuffed shirts. In fact, she had made a point all her life of avoiding them. As a result, she had little idea why they behaved as they did.

Now, though, she had a slight glimmering of understanding. She sharpened her pen, dipped it in the crystal inkwell, and began to scribble furiously.

CHAPTER THREE

Ben extracted a book from a high shelf and flipped it open. The title—*A Country Lady's Diary*—had attracted his interest. He hoped for a treatise on botany or, even better, some discussion of insects. To his disappointment, the book appeared to be a novel about a young woman's attempts to avoid her interfering mother-in-law during the hunting season at a rural estate.

He sighed. It appeared there was little in this immense circulating library but poetry, novels, and satires. So many books, but almost nothing interested him. It was like being at a feast full of foods one could not stomach.

Rather like London.

Come now, he admonished himself. *The situation is not so bad.*

It was not terribly promising, either. True, he seemed to be making amends with Elinor, and if nothing else emerged from this trip, that was a significant accomplishment. It was good to be back in her company. After less than a day, he felt a little of their old camaraderie returning. It would take a long time to repair their ties completely—perhaps it was too much to hope that that could ever happen—but he was on his way.

He still found it hard to forgive Richard Blythe for the way he had spirited Elinor away, leading to such an immense scandal, but he had to admit that it appeared to have worked out for the best. Elinor and her husband seemed very happy together, and their children were sunny-tempered and charming. Elinor was clearly in her element as a grand society hostess, a role she would never have been able to play had she married Lord Penwood, as Ben had urged her to do. He thought he had been doing the right thing at the time.

It appeared that Blythe was doing his best to put the past behind them, and he continued to act with distant courtesy. Even that boisterous sister of his seemed to have resolved to be civil. His face still turned down toward the book in his hands, Ben glanced at Lady Cassandra from the corner of his eye.

She was standing by the large window at the front of the shop. The sunlight pouring through the window glinted off her elegant coiffure. She was speaking to a shorter woman whose mouse-colored hair was pulled back into a simple knot at the back of her head. Neither a curl nor a ribbon enlivened it, and her pale gray dress was similarly plain. Watching the two women conversing was rather like observing a butterfly consorting with a wasp.

As the pair turned toward him, he almost jumped. Returning his gaze to the book, he made such a good show of being absorbed in it that he actually waited until Lady Cassandra spoke his name before raising his eyes.

"I'm sorry," he said, closing the book. "I did not hear you approach."

She glanced down at the volume in his hand. "*A Country Lady's Diary*? You surprise me, Lord Winchfield. I did not imagine you to be a man with a penchant for light novels."

He wasn't, but it irked him somehow to think that she purported to understand him fully on the basis of one day's acquaintance.

"I am a gentleman of hidden depths," he said, startling himself. He was never flippant.

"I'm sure you are," she replied with an enigmatic smile. "May I introduce you to my friend, Miss Anne Lewis?" She nodded toward the pale woman beside her. "Miss Lewis, this is Lord Winchfield."

He extended his hand in greeting but immediately realized the young woman could not see it, as she had shifted her gaze to the floor at his feet.

"Miss Lewis?"

Slowly, she raised her head. "I am pleased to make your acquaintance, m'lord," she said in a voice so faint he could barely hear it.

"And I yours," he murmured. It was like speaking to a nervous puppy. "Do you borrow books from the library often?"

She nodded but said nothing else.

"Are there any in particular that you could recommend?"

She hesitated, then shook her head.

Thank goodness she had spoken when they were introduced, or he would have mistaken her for a mute.

He wracked his brain for another likely topic of conversation. "Have you come to London for the Season, Miss Lewis, or do you live in the capital all year?"

That was a question she could not answer simply with a movement of her head. She seemed to consider it deeply for a moment before saying, "For the Season. Mama wishes me to meet . . . people."

"People?"

The silence stretched for what seemed like an hour before she whispered, "Gentlemen."

"Ah." There seemed to be no other reply. Clearly, they were both in Town with a similar purpose. And she seemed to be the one human in London who had even less enthusiasm for the enterprise than he did.

He hazarded a glance at Lady Cassandra and quickly wished he hadn't. She was biting her lower lip, and he felt a terrible urge to share in the laughter. But that would be most rude to Miss Lewis. It was not her fault she was so abominably shy.

"And you, Lord Winchfield? What brings you to London?"

A note of false brightness in Miss Lewis's voice caught his attention. It was clear that she was trying to pretend she did not know the answer to that question.

He was being manipulated, and not very subtly, by Lady Cassandra. He glared at her, but all that achieved was to induce her to bite down on her lip with more force than before. The woman would be bleeding on the floor before this conversation was over.

"I am here to visit my sister—and, of course, to meet her charming sister-in-law," he added with a nod at Lady Cassandra. "Mainly, I came to London to . . . " How to phrase it without playing directly into Lady Cassandra's hands? To do some scientific research into . . . mating rituals."

The blond woman looked as though she might expire

from the effort of suppressing her laughter. "Excuse me, Miss Lewis, Lord Winchfield. I see a lady on the other side of the room with whom I really must speak." With that, she left him to his fate.

Miss Lewis looked up at him with eyes as round and glassy as a cat's. What was he to do with her?

"Er, what amusements in Town would you recommend? I have only just arrived, and aside from hearing about Almack's—"

"Oh, heavens, do not go to Almack's!" she exclaimed with more force and volume than he'd have thought her capable of.

"Why not? I have been told it is the best place to meet the *ton*."

"It is terrible," she said, her voice once again little more than a whisper. "It is . . . well, it is exactly like being sold at auction."

He blinked. "Really?"

She looked away from him, in the direction in which Lady Cassandra had disappeared. "I should not have said that."

I'm glad you did, he wanted to tell her. *It's the first interesting thing that's popped out of your mouth since we were introduced.*

Instead he said, "I am interested in your honest opinion of the establishment, as I have vouchers to visit next week. You say it is like an auction?"

She nodded as she turned toward him again, with obvious reluctance. "Gentlemen look you up and down as though you were a horse."

"And what about the ladies?"

"They are the same. You hear them in the withdrawing room, giggling about some gentleman's face or hair or clothing. I cannot abide it."

It did not sound like it would be much to Ben's taste, either. But he supposed he would have to run the gauntlet. Elinor had told him that the ambitious mama of every marriageable young woman in the *ton* fought to get tickets to the assembly rooms. It seemed like an efficient way to meet a large number of women at once.

Efficient, but excruciating. He suspected that there would be dancing involved. And while he was a capable enough dancer, he supposed, he had never quite understood the appeal of the activity. If one was going to spend so much time moving about, one might as well be doing something useful, like mending a fence or fixing a roof.

"I cannot blame you," he said in response to Miss Lewis's heartfelt denunciation of Almack's. "I am facing the prospect of attending with much less interest than before."

"Oh, you must not let me dissuade you." She gave a tiny, mirthless laugh. "I am unusual. Most young women adore Almack's."

"Well, I am unusual, too. I know little of dancing and even less of fashion, so I suppose I shall be the chief subject of merriment in the withdrawing rooms when I do make an appearance." He suppressed a frown. What did he care what some gaggle of society misses thought of him? He would be shot of London soon enough. As long as he could find one woman who suited his tastes, the rest of them could go hang.

He suspected quite strongly that Miss Lewis would not be that woman. She was plain and mild, true, but somewhat too mild even for his tastes. However, it would be rude to simply walk away from her in the middle of the shop. He scanned the shelves, looking for something they could discuss, and finally he spotted a

well-worn copy of *Pride and Prejudice*. He had not
read it—not really his sort of thing—but he knew
enough of the plot from overhearing discussions of it at
social occasions to at least start a conversation.

"Have you read *Pride and Prejudice?*" he asked his
companion.

She nodded.

"I have heard it is very good."

Again, her head bobbed.

"Did you like it?"

"Yes."

"Would you say that all of the books by this mysterious author are equally good?"

At this more complex question, her eyes widened.
He was reminded of his initial image of her as a startled puppy. Eventually, she whispered, "Yes."

He was going to have to find a way to repay Lady
Cassandra for giving him the task of amusing this
poor creature. How on earth did anyone as outgoing
as Lady Cassandra become friends with someone as
timid as Miss Lewis? One would think they would
exert a mutual repulsion, like opposing magnetic
charges.

Perhaps, by some wild chance, she knew something
about entomology. "Miss Lewis, are you familiar—"

"Lady Louisa!" she exclaimed in obvious relief as
she looked over his shoulder at someone he could not
see. He turned to follow the direction of her gaze.

"Miss Lewis!" A red-haired woman in an unbe-
coming blue gown and an enormous hat detached
herself from a clot of people nearby and strode toward them. "What a pleasure to see you! But I do not
believe I have made the acquaintance of your friend."
She turned toward him with a friendly smile.

The powers of speech appeared to have deserted Miss Lewis once more. It was as though their brief conversation had used up her allotment of words for the day.

Should he simply introduce himself, he wondered? Was that how things were done here? It certainly wasn't the way they were done in Dorsetshire, but perhaps introducing oneself was like this outlandish coiffure Tyson had given him—a new fashion that hadn't quite made its way to the provinces yet?

He was clearing his throat when he heard Miss Lewis's faint voice making him known to Lady Louisa Dennis. When she was done, he held out his hand to the red-haired woman. "It is my pleasure to meet you."

She took his hand in a firm grip that would have done credit to any gentleman and injury to some. "The pleasure is all mine, my lord. I've been most anxious to make your acquaintance ever since Lady Elinor told me you were coming to Town."

"So you know my sister, then?"

"Oh yes! We've been friends for several years, ever since I made my début. Well, that wasn't so many years ago." She fluttered her eyelashes at him. Apparently, word had already spread through the *ton*, courtesy of Elinor, about his purpose here in Town.

"Do you come to the circulating library often?" he asked Lady Louisa, repeating his opening gambit with Miss Lewis. No sense starting from scratch.

"Almost every week. I am an inveterate reader."

Well, that sounded promising. "What sorts of books do you enjoy?"

"Just about anything, really—novels, biographies, philosophy, scientific texts."

"Science? You wouldn't happen to know anything about botany or entomology, would you?"

"Entomology? That is the study of insects, is it not?"

"Yes." He was impressed.

She shook her head, almost dislodging her precariously balanced hat. "Very little, my lord. My particular fields of interest are chemistry and optics. Do you know anything of Sir Humphrey Davy's efforts to capture images on paper using light and chemicals?"

"I know that he has been largely unsuccessful so far, but beyond that I am ignorant."

"I have several interesting monographs on the subject, should you be interested in borrowing them."

Although the natural world was much more his sphere, he was so intrigued to encounter a female with even a passing knowledge of science that he said, "I might, indeed."

She smiled. "I shall try to remember to bring them with me on Friday."

He frowned. "Friday?"

"That is the date of the rout your sister is holding in your honor, is it not?"

"Yes. It had slipped my mind."

Lady Louisa laughed. "I'm certain Elinor will remind you."

He suddenly remembered the presence of Miss Lewis, and chastised himself for his rudeness at leaving her out of their conversation. "Will you be attending as well, Miss Lewis?"

As soon as the words were out of his mouth, he cursed himself. Perhaps she had not received an invitation! London was nothing like Dorsetshire, where every member of the gentry went to every social event, since neither the number of people nor the number of gatherings was very large.

To his relief, Miss Lewis said, "I have received an invitation, but I am not certain whether I will attend."

"Anne's not terribly comfortable in crowds," Lady Louisa said in a very loud stage whisper that was likely audible to Miss Lewis as well as anyone else within twenty feet.

He smiled at the shy young woman. "You will be most welcome if you do attend." It wasn't that he wanted to see her, really, as much as he wanted to ensure she did not feel left out.

"Thank you," she whispered.

It seemed as good an opportunity as any to move along. He did not want to spend too much time with any one lady until he'd had a chance to fully gauge her character. He'd learned in the past that women were apt to take even casual conversations with earls very deeply to heart. "I suspect my sister and her sister-in-law are looking for me, so I shall take my leave. It was a pleasure to have met you both, and I look forward to renewing our acquaintance on Friday."

The two women bid him farewell, and he strode quickly through the library in search of Elinor. To his surprise, he realized that his palms were damp. Why on earth should he be nervous speaking to two completely innocuous females?

He supposed it was the novelty of speaking to persons he did not know. Since inheriting his title eleven years ago, he had spent most of his time at the estate, keeping up repairs or doing research, or in the close-knit social world of Dorsetshire and the surrounding counties. It was rare for him to encounter more than one stranger or two in any given week.

Perhaps this trip to London would be fruitful in more ways than one. He was a bit young, he reflected, to have become a hermit.

"You should have seen poor Ben this morning! He looked like a hare run to ground by the hounds." Elinor turned from the escritoire in her private sitting room, where she was reviewing menus from Cook for dinner the next day.

"He should have expected as much." Richard folded his lanky form onto the small chaise in front of the fire. "Some rich earl no one's ever seen suddenly showing up in London? It's like feeding time at the chicken coop." He patted the empty space beside him on the chaise. "Come over here and sit with me."

Elinor knew exactly where sitting with Richard would lead, and she had matters of importance to discuss with her husband before she became distracted.

"I need to finish these menus first. And don't dismiss Ben's troubles so quickly. He truly looked distraught, at least until Lady Louisa Dennis showed up. I cannot believe Cassandra thought he and Miss Lewis should suit. Miss Lewis! She's a dear, but she's afraid of her own shadow. If she finds a match at all this Season, I shall go about on Oxford Street in last year's hat."

"That's a pretty daring wager. Last year's hat! I'd be shocked beyond words."

Elinor smiled. She was well used to her husband's mockery.

"But in all seriousness, what am I to do about Ben?"

"Do? What do you mean?" Richard stretched his

hand along the curved back of the chaise. "He has stated that he wants a plain, quiet wife. Granted, I know 'plain' and 'quiet' aren't two of the adjectives I would associate most closely with the ladies in your circle, but surely there is someone—"

"That's just it," Elinor said.

"That's just what?" Richard was wearing that expression of utter confusion that always made her smile.

"The problem. Ben says he wants a plain, quiet wife."

"That seems reasonable to me. Wouldn't be my taste, or else I would not have married you—"

She tossed a crumpled piece of paper in his direction.

"But it isn't such a strange request. Many gentlemen want little more out of marriage than a partnership with a mild woman who will leave them alone."

"But not Ben. He deserves more than that."

Richard let out an exasperated sigh. "But he doesn't *want* more than that, Elinor. Why do you Rowlands feel you must control everything and everyone—even other Rowlands?"

She grinned. "I like to think of it as fostering and encouraging, rather than controlling. Just pointing people in the direction that they would move in themselves, if their vision weren't clouded."

"And what makes you think your brother's vision is clouded? If you ask me, he's a fairly decisive sort. He certainly made up his mind quickly enough about me, all those years ago." Richard stood up from the chaise and crossed the room to stand behind her chair. He laid his hands on her shoulders, and rubbed the spot on the back of her neck that he knew often ached when she sat at her desk for long periods. She closed her eyes in relaxation for a moment, but then remembered she wanted to discuss this matter further with her husband, and opened them again.

"He thinks he wants someone plain and quiet because of us. The elopement, the scandal, all of that."

Richard's hands fell away from her shoulders. "Surely he isn't still thinking about that? It was more than a decade ago. People have long ago moved on to talk of other things. Certainly no one in the *ton* cuts us because of it. If the high-in-the-instep Lady Jersey can forgive us, then certainly—"

Elinor raised her hand to stop this tirade, which she had heard in various forms so often that she could repeat the key phrases by heart. "Darling, I'm sorry I brought it up. But the fact remains that Ben—wrongly, I will agree with you—still harbors an unholy fear of anything that seems even slightly unconventional. We spoke about this a little last night, after you and Cassandra had retired. He is convinced that a quiet woman would suit him best."

"And you do not share his view."

"No. He thinks all lively women—myself excepted, of course—are flighty and foolish. He has a lot of intellectual interests, and he doesn't want to marry someone who can talk of nothing but fashion and gossip."

"That's understandable. Who would? But he doesn't have to marry a bluestocking just to find a female capable of carrying on an intelligent conversation."

"He thinks he does. I think there's more to the story than he is telling me, but I can't guess at what."

"Whatever it is, it is his business."

Elinor puffed out a loud breath. She loved Richard dearly, but sometimes he could be so obtuse.

"No, darling, it's my business, too. He's my brother—the only close family I have left. I have to help him."

"You, Elinor, feel you have to help everyone. What about helping your poor, tired husband?" Still standing behind her, he lifted a hand to her cheek and ran one finger slowly down the side of her neck. It was most distracting.

"Richard?"

"Mmm?"

"I have just the perfect match for Ben, if only he—and she—could see it."

"Who?" His voice could not have evinced less interest if she had been speaking of flower arrangements or silk slippers, but she suspected her answer would get his attention.

"Cassandra."

His finger abruptly stopped its rather delightful meanderings. "*Our* Cassandra?"

"The very one."

He stepped back from her and sat down with a thump on a small ottoman beside her desk. "I believe I need to get you away from London, my dear. The stale air in Town seems to have affected your brain."

"My brain is perfectly fine, as well you know. Just listen to me. Cassandra has been saying for some months now that all the men she knows, except for Perry, are foolish fribbles—"

"Perhaps if she sought out men more for their sense than for their ability to turn a witty phrase, she would not find all men in London so woefully lacking in gravity."

"But see, there's the thing!" Elinor leaned forward to press her point home. "Ben has plenty of sense, *and* wit as well."

Richard blinked. "Wit? Winchfield? I don't believe he would know the meaning of the term without consulting one of his demmed dictionaries."

"Richard, don't be cruel. It doesn't suit you." Elinor pushed a stray lock of hair out of her eyes. "You met Ben when he was at his worst. Our father was recently deceased, and Ben was feeling rather overwhelmed with all the responsibilities of the estate. He must have seemed rather grim to you."

"Still does." Richard's voice was mulish.

"But you should have known him when we were children. Granted, he was never theatrical—I don't think, for instance, that he would last ten minutes in the bow window at White's—but he had a very sly sense of humor. He used to do a most amusing impression of our French tutor, for instance. And he was very good at poking fun at himself."

"As far as I have observed, he seems to have completely lost that facility."

"You don't know him as I once knew him," Elinor insisted. "There is more to Ben than meets the eye."

"I maintain that a man can change a great deal in ten years, and that he may well have left those childish tendencies behind forever. But let us say that Winchfield is, in fact, a secret Sheridan. That still leaves us with the other half of the equation: Cassandra."

"But what of Cassandra?" It was Elinor's turn to be perplexed.

"You may claim to be the expert on Winchfield, but I fancy I know my sister as well as anyone does. And

I believe that your brother—no offense intended—would be the last sort of man she would ever consider for a husband."

"No offense taken. But why?"

Richard toyed with a small dish on the table beside him, seeming to gather his thoughts. "Cassandra has always been drawn to glittery sorts of men—the sort of gentlemen who gather others around them," he said at last. "Leaders and wits. Remember the year she was so smitten with Lord Kerrisdale?"

Elinor frowned. "Heavens, yes. He may be a talented poet—although I'd be the last one to be a useful judge on that score—but he was a terrible excuse for a human being."

"I agree, but those are the sorts of men who attract her eye. And why not? She may have been out for several Seasons now, but she is still widely regarded as an Incomparable." Richard delivered this last statement with no little pride, as though he himself had played a role in making Cassandra a celebrated beauty. Men always wanted to take credit for everything, Elinor thought. Sometimes, it was just easier to let them.

"But when she gets to know Ben, she will see that he is just the sort of man of substance she has been seeking." Elinor waved a hand as if brushing off further discussion. "I have no worries about Cassandra. She is a sensible woman, and I know she is getting somewhat tired of the Marriage Mart and all that it entails. The difficult part will be convincing Ben of the wisdom of my plan."

"*I* am not convinced of the wisdom of your plan."

She laughed. "It's obvious that Cassandra would be ideal for Ben. She is intelligent and sensible, and beautiful as well."

"Yes, beautiful. Do you not think that will be enough to dissuade your brother? Aside from the fact that never, in anyone's imagination, could she be classified as either quiet or meek."

Elinor raised her eyebrows. "Well, that *is* true. But it is as I say—Ben doesn't really want a milk-and-water miss. He just thinks he does."

"Well, I wish you luck in convincing him of your theory. We tried to convince him of something once before, in case you've forgotten. We had no luck in that case either. If our powers of persuasion had been better, we would not have been forced to elope."

"But surely he sees now that he was wrong. After all, look how content we are."

"I might be a little more content, Lady Elinor, if you would pay attention to the very obvious hints I've been sending you since the moment I walked in this door." He stood up and moved toward her chair, then rested his hands once more on the tops of her shoulders. Then he lowered his head and kissed her gently on the side of her neck. "It is still an hour until dinner. Do you think we might cease talk of Winchfield and Cassandra for at least part of that period, and move on to more interesting things?"

Elinor closed her eyes and leaned back toward her husband. "Yes, darling, I think we might."

CHAPTER FOUR

Ben glanced around the sweltering drawing room in consternation. He would not have believed so many people could fit into his sister's elegant salon. There must have been more than one hundred people packed into the room and its adjoining corridor, plus uncounted numbers in the tiny garden and the foyer. He glanced out one of the high windows into Berkeley Square to see a crush of carriages that stretched in all directions.

"Good Lord," he muttered as he swiped his hand over the perspiration beading his forehead. "It's like race day at Newmarket."

"If you're seeking someone to talk to, you don't have to settle for yourself," a voice said behind him. He turned to see Lady Cassandra, her arms crossed and her eyes alight with humor.

"You have caught me in a very bad habit. This is what comes of living alone in the wilds of Dorsetshire for ten years, with naught but some dogs and several ant colonies for company."

"Ant colonies?" she asked, coming to stand beside him and looking down on the chaos below. He caught a whiff of lavender—from her dress or from her hair, he could not tell. It was a plant he had once examined in great detail, so the scent was one of the few he could identify. He had always liked it.

"Yes. I study them."

She let the curtain fall and turned to face him once more. "Study ants? Is there that much to know about them?"

He knew from experience that most people did not truly want to know anything about ants when they asked such questions. They were simply being polite. "They have a society all their own, with leaders and followers, projects and disasters," he said, as he always did, knowing that she would be happy to leave it at that.

"Projects? What sorts of projects does an ant execute? I would think avoiding human feet would be occupation enough for a lifetime."

"Do you really want to know?"

She laughed. "I'm not sure. Is it gruesome?"

He felt an answering smile on his face. "Not at all. Mostly, they maintain their nests and gather food."

"What do they eat?"

"Vegetable matter, fruit, dead bugs—"

"You promised this wouldn't be gruesome."

He laughed. "Didn't you ever wonder where all the dead bugs go? Why we aren't up to our knees in them?"

"I must confess, I have never given the matter a moment's thought."

"Not surprising. Myrmexology isn't a common topic of drawing room conversation."

"Mer . . . well, whatever it was you said, I'm assuming that's the study of ants. Unless it's the study of dead bugs."

"No, you were correct the first time. *Myrmex* is the

Greek word for ant, and *myrmexology* is a word I made up to describe the study of ants."

"If I were American, I would ask whether it concerns uncles as well."

"I beg your pardon?" He could not seem to become accustomed to Lady Cassandra's conversational leaps.

"Ants. That is how some of them pronounce the word that we say 'aunts.' So to them, an ant colony would be a houseful of elderly women." She paused, then added with a mischievous smile, "Elderly women dunking dead crickets in their tea."

The image struck him as so funny that he let out a bark of laughter. As he did, several people turned to stare at the odd sound. Apparently realizing they were ogling the guest of honor, they quickly turned back to their previous conversations.

Good God, it had been so long since he'd laughed that he seemed to have forgotten how.

"Lady Cassandra! So this is where you've been hiding yourself—over here in the folds of the draperies." Two gentlemen separated themselves from the throng and walked toward them. Both were dressed in expertly tailored coats and windblown-looking neckcloths that Ben supposed were the latest stare of fashion. He wished Tyson were in the room to witness his employer even conversing with such pinks of the *ton*. His valet would be pleased.

"I haven't been hiding at all," Ben's companion said with a low chuckle. "It's simple enough to become invisible by accident in this crush. Elinor is well known for her soirées, of course, but even this crowd is exceptional."

"Nothing like a rich bachelor earl to bring out the ladies," remarked the shorter of the two men with a

smirk. "Would that I had such a title and such a fortune! I should be the most popular man in London,
even if I had the face of a pug and the demeanor of a
bulldog."

"Yes, and the personal habits of an elderly spaniel!"
replied his companion, a good-looking man of about
Ben's height.

Lady Cassandra smiled. "Well, then, you will be
most pleased to meet our guest of honor. I assure you
that he bears no resemblance to any known canine."

The taller man had the good grace to flush. "Beg
your pardon, my lord," he said, bowing as Lady Cassandra introduced him as Mr. Peregrine Russell and
his friend as Mr. Edward Symes.

"We've run into the most amusing gentleman,"
Symes said to Lady Cassandra when the introductions were done. "He is newly arrived in Town after a
trip to the Canadas, and you simply must meet him.
He has such incredible stories about bears!"

"Yes, do join us, Cass—Lady Cassandra," said Russell, laying a hand on her arm. "You will adore him, I
assure you." He paused and glanced toward Ben. "You
are most welcome to join us, Lord Winchfield."

"Thank you, sir, but I believe I have engaged a lady
for the first dance after the musicians return from
their rest. I really should go seek her out." He was
fairly certain this was not a lie, but he had long ago
lost track of whom he had engaged and when. He was
trusting Elinor to keep him on his toes.

The little party departed, and Ben watched their
progress across the room. As they went, other gentlemen joined them, like flies drawn to a dish of honey.

Drawn to Lady Cassandra, he suspected. She was
at the center of the lively group as it finally came to

a stop near the fireplace. Occasionally, he could hear her laughter pealing across the room.

It was no wonder she attracted such attention, he thought as he leaned against the wall. She was easily the most beautiful woman in the room tonight. What he knew about women's fashions would fit on the head of a pin with room to spare, but whatever the fabric was of the dress she wore, it suited her admirably. It was a deep blue that made her blond hair seem even brighter and shinier in contrast. The wide, square neckline and tiny short sleeves showed off her shoulders and arms—and much else—to advantage. He couldn't see her jewels from this distance, but he remembered the simple yet elegant sapphires that had sparkled at her throat and in her ears, likely Blythe family heirlooms.

He felt a hand on his arm and looked away from the little crowd across the room into his sister's face. "Oh, hello, Ellie. Please forgive me. I did not hear you approach."

"I'm not surprised. The noise in here is exceptional. When I invited half of London to the party, I hardly expected everyone to make an appearance."

"Well, the dog-faced Earl of Winchfield is apparently considered quite the prize." Ben was surprised at how much the two men's careless gibes had rankled. It was not so much that he resented being compared to a dog—most of the dogs he knew had better personalities than people did—it was that he disliked being defined solely by his name and the size of his purse.

"I beg your pardon?"

He shook his head. "I'm just being foolish. Thank you for organizing this lovely party on such short notice."

She grinned. "I don't need an excuse to be social,

you know that. But I'm glad you are enjoying it. I'm
here to remind you that you are promised to Miss
Ogilvy for the next dance. The musicians will be
ready to play again in a few minutes."

"Am I? Thank you. Now, which one is Miss
Ogilvy?" He began scanning the room, his gaze
alighting against his will on the small group by the
fireplace again. It appeared to have grown, but Lady
Cassandra was still at its center.

Just as Georgina had always been.

"You should ask her to dance," Elinor said.

"Who? Miss Ogilvy? I thought I already had." Hell's
bells, did *all* the social rules in London differ from
those in Dorsetshire, or was it just his imagination?

"No, you dullard." Elinor's voice was warm with
affection—warmth he did not deserve after the
abominable way he had treated her all these years.
"Everything is arranged with Miss Ogilvy. I meant
Cassandra."

"Lady Cassandra!" He laughed. "She is as far from
my orbit as the sun is from the earth."

"Now I will call you a dullard in earnest! She is
no better born than we."

"Perhaps we are alike in social status, but just
look." He nodded across the room. "She is an Incomparable, and I am just a countryman with naught
to offer but a name and an estate."

Elinor shook her head. "How have you come to
think so little of yourself? You did not hold such a low
opinion when we were children."

"Children grow up to be adults and learn the ways
of the world. Believe me, Lady Cassandra is the last
sort of woman whose affections I would desire to en-

gage. I have told you that I am seeking a plain, meek female."

"Yes you have, although heaven knows why. But all this is beside the point. I'm not asking you to offer for her, for heaven's sake. I'm just suggesting you ask her to dance. Won't it be a relief to dance with someone you know you don't have to evaluate as a potential marriage partner?" His sister smiled. "And I happen to know that Cassandra is an excellent dancer. It would be fun."

Well, he had to admit that it would be pleasant to have at least one dance during which his partner did not launch into a long and detailed inventory of her charms and her family's status. With Lady Cassandra, there would be no pretense that anything more than a dance was taking place.

"You do have a point," he told his sister, and did not miss the tiny smile of triumph his words elicited. Elinor was obviously avid for him to dance with her sister-in-law, for reasons he could not fathom. When they had been children, Elinor had shown a marked delight in trying to manipulate others to her wishes— from their father, who had acquiesced all too easily to his beloved daughter's suggestions, to the head groom, who more often than not would let her take short turns around the paddock on their father's forbidden mount. Elinor loved being able to control people, but he couldn't fault her for that. It was something of a Rowland family trait.

"Very well. Come, I shall reacquaint you with Miss Ogilvy, who is as plain as a barn door and should suit your odd tastes admirably. But first, let us see if Cassandra has any open dances."

Ben rather doubted that she would. Hopeful of a reprieve, he trailed across the room in his sister's wake.

"I almost did not recognize Lady Louisa without her hat," Perry said, looking across the room at said lady, who was wearing a dun-colored dress that did nothing to flatter her. "It is the only way I am able to pick her out of a crowd in the street. Indoors, she almost blends into the furniture."

"*I* did not even realize that her hair was red," Edward Symes chimed in. "That must be why she is such a good client for the Oxford Street milliners. It's a shame, really, that dye is so outré. There should be a special dispensation in Parliament for such extreme cases."

"I can see the newspaper headlines now, should such a proposal ever come before the House of Lords: HEIRS SPLIT HAIRS."

"DYING FOR A NOBLE CAUSE."

"PEERS PONDER PIGMENTS."

Cassandra laughed, feeling a bit unkind as she did so. Lady Louisa was not one of her favorite people—she found her brash and self-serving, and really could not imagine why Elinor put up with her—but for some reason Perry and Edward's repartee struck her tonight as unkind. "Really, if the two of you would put those quick minds to some higher purpose, you might actually accomplish something in life."

"Ah, but that's what boring Cits do—accomplish things," Edward protested. "We are here merely to keep life light. Everyone has a calling. We don't fight ours."

"And you do it so very well," she said, feeling churlish for chiding them. She favored Edward with a smile, and he grinned back in response. He was really so amusing. It was a shame she felt nothing for him but sisterly affection.

But as for Perry—well, she would be quite willing to entertain any sort of romantic interest he might show. Unfortunately, he had not evinced one whit of fascination for her, or any other female, since they had first met years ago.

"I don't believe I'm suited for marriage, and since I am the fourth son of a baronet, no one can force me into it," he'd told her once. "'Tis quite fortunate for everyone, actually. I'd make a dreadful husband, since I've no talent for managing money, no interest in politics and a morbid fear of children." That final remark had done much to nip Cassandra's romantic fantasies about her friend in the bud, but it hadn't eradicated them entirely. Secretly, she rather hoped she could change his mind about the joys of raising a family.

"Ho, here comes your friend, the country earl," said Edward. "Did your partner fail to materialize, Winchfield?" he asked as Elinor and her brother joined them.

"Not at all," Lord Winchfield replied in his low, well-modulated baritone. "I am on my way to collect her now, as I believe the musicians are just about to resume their places. But as I was passing, I thought I would ask"—he glanced back at his sister, who nodded—"I thought I would ask you, Lady Cassandra, if you might reserve a dance for me."

Elinor had most certainly put her brother up to this, Cassandra saw. But if her sister-in-law intended a bit of matchmaking, she would be disappointed. Lord Winchfield cut a fine figure, certainly, but aside from that admitted advantage, he was the last sort of man she would consider as a suitor. Not only did he spend

his days studying bugs—good heavens—but he had
not one shred of wit about him. She'd even had to explain her little ant pun to him.

Besides, he made no secret of the fact that he intended to return to Dorsetshire the moment he had
succeeded in finding, wooing, and marrying a plain,
meek female. Cassandra would be as lost in Dorsetshire as she would be in the wilds of the Canadas that
Edward's acquaintance had just described to them.
Anything more than a day's journey from London
seemed to her heathen territory. She went to the country, of course—for the hunt, for the races at Ascot, for
Christmas celebrations. But the country as a place to
live, all year round? She could not fathom such madness. Why would one choose to spend one's days
rusticating among the cornfields when one could have
the grand homes of Mayfair, the shops of Oxford
Street, and the riding paths of Hyde Park at one's
doorstep? It struck her as choosing to live in purgatory
when St. Peter had already opened the pearly gates and
admitted one to heaven. Surely Elinor knew her better
than to try to match her with a countryman?

Cassandra suddenly realized that the earl was
awaiting her response to his request. Even Perry, Edward, and the other gentlemen in her circle had fallen
silent. She would have to say yes. She had already
told Perry that she had left the waltz at the end of the
evening open. Despite herself, she'd hoped that he
would ask her for it. He had not, however. As a result, it would seem rude in the extreme to turn down
the invitation of the guest of honor and her relative
by marriage. She didn't flatter herself, but she knew
that her words and actions carried social weight. If

she appeared to cut the earl, it might hurt his standing among the *ton*. *Botheration*.

"I have no engagement for the last waltz, my lord, and I would be most happy to have you as my partner. Thank you," she said.

"A waltz?" His voice was dubious.

Cassandra had a terrible thought. Perhaps he did not know the dance? After all, it had only become acceptable in London recently. In Dorsetshire, for all she knew, people still favored the minuet.

"Yes."

"Thank you, I would be honored. Until then, my lady. Gentlemen." He bowed and took his leave.

As she watched his retreating back, Cassandra resigned herself to a spin about the floor during which she would likely learn more about the secret life of insects than she'd ever dreamed of asking. She repressed a sigh and turned back toward her friends with a wide smile. They must never guess that she wasn't delighted by the prospect of dancing with the earl. She had promised Elinor to be kind to Lord Winchfield, and she was determined to keep to her promise. Even if her feet paid the price.

"Well, that should end your evening on an uplifting note," Perry murmured in her ear.

"I am honored to dance with Lord Winchfield." Her voice sounded stiff even in her own ears.

"Whatever for? You certainly don't need his money or his title. You do not lack for suitors. And you do not strike me as the Country Countess type."

"Perry, be quiet. It is only a dance, not a lifetime commitment."

"Thank providence for that gentle mercy."

She did, in actual fact. But it was cruel of Perry to

state it so baldly. He seemed in particularly acidic form tonight, and Cassandra found it unappealing.

"Why are you defending him, anyway?" Perry asked. "When Elinor initially announced his visit, you bent my ear for half an hour, telling me that he had treated your sister-in-law terribly and did not deserve her regard, nor yours."

"I have changed my mind." She hadn't, not really, but she said so for Elinor's sake.

Perry's voice was thick with disbelief. "You? I have known you for four years, Cassandra, and I have never known you to change your mind about anything."

Was she really so set in her ways, Cassandra wondered as the conversation moved into other channels. It wouldn't be surprising, she thought as she listened to her friends' repartee about the party guests with half an ear. Most women her age were married and mothers by her age. Settled. Adults. Why did she feel so unsettled all of a sudden, then?

It must be the earl's arrival that had so discomfited her. All this effort to pretend she liked him was enervating. The sooner she could help him find a suitable green girl, the sooner he would leave and she could resume her usual entertainments. She scanned the room with an eagle eye. There must be someone here who would do.

She saw Elinor leading her brother over to Mary Ogilvy. Oh yes, Mary was completely inoffensive and as innocent as a child. Excellent choice.

Near the dais she spotted another clot of young women with their mamas. She must remember to ask Elinor which of those skittish colts had been introduced to the earl. With that resolution in mind, she turned back to Edward Symes, who was regaling the group with a long story about Prinny's tailor.

Ben held up his hand and Lady Cassandra put hers into it. Her hand was small, warm, and very soft. "Shall we?"

She nodded, nibbling slightly on her lower lip. She probably thought he couldn't dance. He couldn't blame her—he certainly wasn't as urbane as most of the other gentlemen here.

He rested his hand on her small waist as her palm settled on his shoulder. "See? I know how we are to stand. I promise you, Lady Cassandra, I shall not embarrass you unduly."

She smiled. "Was my unease so obvious?"

"A little," he said as the opening bars of the music began and they began to move across the gleaming parquet floor. Unlike most of the young women he had partnered tonight, in the waltz and other dances, she felt as light as air in his arms. Again, he caught the faint scent of lavender.

"I do apologize. I just thought, seeing as you rarely get to London—"

"Even in Dorsetshire, we have a small veneer of civilization," he said, smiling to take the sting from his words. "The winters are long and we must amuse ourselves in some fashion. A kind neighbor taught me the dance so that I might properly hold up my head at the Winchfield assemblies. 'Twouldn't do, after all, for the lord of the manor to think himself above the latest fashion."

Lady Cassandra smiled, and her whole face lit up, her blue eyes sparking in her heart-shaped face. She truly was an Incomparable—just the sort, dash it, who had always attracted his interest. He felt goose-flesh prickling along his arms and the back of his neck.

Do not give the idea one moment's consideration, he told himself. *Women like Lady Cassandra Blythe lead only to disappointment and scandal.*

"Did you have a chance to meet Miss Fielding?" his companion asked, nodding toward a plump young woman who was dancing with Richard Blythe.

"Yes. Her mother approached Elinor not long after they arrived to request an introduction. The young lady seems a quiet sort."

"She cannot help it. It is almost impossible for her—indeed, for anyone—to say a word in the presence of Mrs. Fielding. 'Tis a shame women cannot stand for Parliament, as she would be able to talk to any bill at such length that the rest of the members would pass it in self-defense." She smiled as they spun by the dais, where the excellent musicians were working hard.

"Surely she cannot be so bad?"

"Believe me, I have sat opposite her at dinner only to realize I had not said a word between the soup and the sweet." Cassandra paused. "I do not mean to dissuade you from the daughter, however. She is as gentle as her mother is unpleasant. I just hope she is not too placid for your tastes. If you were seeking someone a bit more lively—"

"No, truly. Thank you for your help, but I'm afraid I'm not a very lively man, and anyone too effervescent would quickly be bored of me."

She raised her eyebrows. "If you are to succeed in the Marriage Mart, you must learn to proclaim your virtues and be more circumspect about your faults."

"I'm just being honest." He sought a way to turn the conversation away from himself. "I am sorry that your friend Miss Lewis did not attend. Or perhaps I did not see her?" He executed a quick turn between two pairs of dancers who had stopped for a moment of conversation, and breathed a sigh of relief when the quick movement didn't cause his partner to stumble.

"No, you are correct. She did not come." Cassandra gave him a small smile. "I am sorry that I left you two alone at the library the other day. I wanted to give you a chance to get acquainted, but I know how difficult it can be to talk with Miss Lewis."

"I appreciated your efforts on my behalf," he said. "It might not have been a rollicking discussion, but we managed."

"I have tried my best to encourage her to be more social, but I confess that it is rather like trying to write with a dull pen that is beyond sharpening. Nothing I say seems to make the slightest bit of difference."

"It seems surprising that you and she are friends at all. You seem as different as chalk and cheese."

"I suppose we are." Cassandra released her hold on his shoulder for a moment to push a stray curl out of her eyes. "Her mother and mine were once fast friends, and Mama asked me to watch out for her here in London. In truth, Miss Lewis is avid to return to the country as quickly as possible. She cannot abide London. That is why I rather thought you and she would be congenial."

He smiled. "I have not the talent to bring her out of her shell, I'm afraid."

"The most skilled chef in all of London likely

could not manage that feat. I do not think the tools have yet been invented."

Ben looked down into his partner's lovely face. "That seems unnecessarily nasty. True, Miss Lewis is very shy, and it can be difficult to maintain a conversation with her, but that does not mean she should be held up to ridicule."

"I was not ridiculing her. I was merely stating a fact."

"But in a way designed to generate laughter."

Lady Cassandra tilted her head to one side. "Is laughter wrong, back in Dorsetshire?"

"No. There are many who amuse themselves at the expense of others, even in a village as small as Winchfield. I just do not think it seemly."

"Forgive me for saying so, my lord, but things are different here in London. One's social status rises and falls on one's wit."

"Only on wit? Not on wealth, intelligence, or generosity?"

"Those things are important, certainly. But among the people I know, wit is the most precious currency."

"Perhaps, Lady Cassandra, it is you who leads the sheltered life, not I."

In his arms, she stiffened. "Lord Winchfield, I do not believe it is your place to comment on my life, particularly since you have just chastised me for criticizing other people's."

"I did not make my observation to be cruel, and I apologize for offending you." He suppressed a groan. Could he not have one conversation in London without sticking both feet in his mouth? "I was merely, as a friend, pointing out a habit that is somewhat ungentle, in the hope that you might find the information useful. I know that I would be glad to be told of any unpleasant habits of which I was un-aware."

She grimaced. "Would you be interested in knowing, my lord, that you are the most arrogant man it has been my misfortune to dance with this evening—perhaps any evening?"

"Arrogant?" he said. "Because I deign to criticize the Incomparable Lady Cassandra?"

"Because you seem to think you know best in all things, and that the world should operate according to your dictates."

"I never said that."

"You implied it. I should have known as much, after the way you treated Elinor." She looked behind her as they narrowly avoided colliding with Lady Louisa and her partner.

"What do you know of the way I treated Elinor? You were not there."

"I know that you tried to prevent her from marrying Richard, thinking you knew best."

"I will admit that I tried to arrange a marriage between my sister and Viscount Penwood." And what a disaster that had been. He still felt ill as he remembered the night Penwood had asked for his blessing and then gone into the conservatory at Winchfield Hall to offer for Elinor. When the viscount had emerged, he'd announced that Elinor had accepted him. Ben had been so pleased that he had not stopped to wonder why Elinor herself had not come out to share this good news with him.

To this day, he berated himself for announcing the betrothal to the small supper party that had gathered in their home that night, instead of waiting to hear the news directly from his sister. When he'd learned that

Penwood had lied, it had been too late to repair the damage. Elinor had felt she had no choice but to flee to Gretna Green with Blythe.

"You acted without taking her feelings into account," Lady Cassandra said now, her voice sharp with indignation.

"Perhaps I was wrong, but I acted from the best of intentions." His words sounded petulant, even in his own ears, so he tried to explain further. "Our family had known Lord Penwood's for five generations. Elinor and I had grown up alongside him. He had an unstained name, a good income, and a rich estate. Your brother, meanwhile, was a mystery to me. I knew only what I could observe in our chance meetings, and what Elinor told me. And what she told me did not recommend him highly."

"And what was that?"

Dash it, how had their amicable dance degenerated into a rehashing of all the old grievances he had been so determined to put behind him? "Surely, if Elinor told you what an ogre I'd been, she also told you that I thought Richard a high-living Corinthian who would never provide a stable life for her?"

"Perhaps it was just that you feared she would move away and leave you to rot in Dorsetshire alone?"

It was all Ben could do not to flinch, as that arrow pierced him a little too near the heart. "That was her affair. Granted, if she had married Penwood, she would have become mistress of Penwood Park, which lies just a half hour ride from Winchfield Hall."

"How convenient." She puffed out a breath in apparent exasperation. "I'm sorry, my lord. I keep resolving to be civil, but then my resentment regarding your treatment of Elinor keeps bubbling up to wash away all my good intentions." She looked up into his face with a pleading expression, as though willing him to understand her harsh judgment. "It is just that Elinor is so dear to me. She is such a good-natured soul—far more so than I, I'm afraid—and it makes me sad to think that she was ever put through any anguish."

"But I did have Ellie's best interests at heart, truly." On this issue, above all others, it was hard to withstand the criticism of people who had not been there. No one but he knew how difficult it had been, at twenty, to find himself the sole arbiter of his sister's future. Never had he so devoutly wished, before or since, that their father had not passed so early and left Ben to play both sibling and parent in their guardian's absence.

"And, interestingly, the interests you ascribed to Elinor coincided precisely with yours." Her frown showed that her determination to be polite to him had almost vanished.

As had his desire to be civil to her. He was trying, but she was making it damnably difficult. "So you believe. I suspect that nothing I can say will change your mind. And perhaps it is not surprising that you are biased against me. After all, if I had succeeded in my efforts to have Elinor marry Penwood, your brother would have failed in his own efforts to wed her himself. I can see where familial loyalty would cloud your judgment."

"Arrogant *and* condescending!" Abruptly, Lady Cassandra stopped moving, almost pitching him off his feet and causing several other dancers to shoot them dark glances. "My judgment is perfectly clear, Lord Winchfield. You did not wish Elinor and Richard to marry because that was an outcome you had not desired, engineered, or approved. You cannot bear the idea of the rest of the world not moving to the beat of your drummer."

He dropped her hand and stepped away. "Since you appear to have decided who I am and what I think beyond the point of debate, there is really no point in continuing this conversation or this dance, is there?" What was it about this woman that spurred him to such depths of anger? He liked to think of himself as an equable man who rarely gave into fits of temper.

"Do you wish to cause a scene, my lord?"

He looked around the room and saw that several people seated on gilt chairs at the edges of the dance floor were whispering to each other and regarding him and Lady Cassandra with avid interest. For the first time, he had some inkling of how his ants must feel when he examined them with a magnifying glass.

He sighed and seized Lady Cassandra's hand again. "You are right, I suppose. The last thing I want to do is embarrass Elinor. So let us proceed."

"Try to restrain your enthusiasm."

"Try to restrain your sarcasm."

The last minutes of the dance were excruciating. He spun them around mechanically, avoiding Lady Cassandra's eyes as she avoided his. The moment the music ended, they dropped their hands. He bowed as she curtsied, then he led her to an empty chair near the window. The walk across the emptying dance floor felt like a mile, and his legs felt as though they were made of rusted iron.

"I hope that, if nothing else, you will have fun mocking me to your fine friends," he said as he left.

"I hope it isn't too lonely for you, up there on your high horse."

He bowed again and took his leave. He had never been so glad to turn his back on a dance partner, and it astonished him to think that he had felt even a slight frisson of interest in her at the beginning of the dance. He had been right to warn himself away from her. Women like Lady Cassandra were, indeed, only conduits to scandal and embarrassment.

CHAPTER FIVE

"More sugar, Lady Cassandra?" Lord Winchfield's voice was icily polite.

"No, thank you." Would he and Richard never leave? Morosely, Cassandra nibbled on a piece of bacon as her brother and their guest spoke about horses. They planned a trip to Tattersall's this morning, and she heartily wished they would finish their meals and depart.

"If you don't hurry, all the best horses will be gone," she muttered.

Richard raised his eyebrows, as well he might. "Not even the most eager gentlemen will be there for at least another half hour."

Cassandra made a show of glancing at the carriage clock on the mantel. "My apologies. I thought the hour was later than it is." She stood up and crossed the room toward the sideboard to help herself to another poached egg, hoping her movement would dissuade her brother from further conversation. She really did not feel like speaking to anyone today.

She stood over the silver chafing dish, realizing that she didn't really want anything else to eat. After an almost sleepless night, she felt weak and queasy, and she had hoped that food might settle her stomach.

But now that she was at the sideboard, she could barely look at the morsels on display.

She put the cover back on the chafing dish and hoped that neither Richard nor the earl would notice that her plate was still empty when she returned to the table.

Her worries were unnecessary. The two men were deep in a discussion of the merits of various horse breeders. They ignored her, which suited her entirely. Within five minutes, she had finished her tea and was about to leave when Elinor swept into the room.

"Ellie!" Richard exclaimed, rising from his chair and kissing his wife on the cheek. "We are all up and about early today. I did not expect to see you before ĵoon, given all the hard work you did yesterday."

"Yes, thank you again, Elinor," Lord Winchfield said as he stood. "I am touched that you went to so much trouble to help me make my metaphorical debut."

Elinor grinned as she took a seat. "It was no sacrifice. The rout will be the talk of the *ton* this week, and that can't help but burnish my reputation as a hostess." A little maid bustled over with a china teapot, poured a cup for her mistress, and set the pot on the table before curtsying and leaving the room. She glanced at the sideboard. "Have you three early risers left me anything to eat?"

"I believe so." Cassandra dredged up a smile for her sister-in-law. Just because she was furious with Elinor's brother didn't mean she had to visit her foul mood on everyone else. "Try the scones. Cook did a particularly fine job this morning."

To her relief, the gentlemen seemed to take Elinor's arrival as their cue to exit. "We are off to Tattersall's this morning, my dear," Richard said. "I have also promised to take Winchfield to Weston. He was much taken with the coats some of the gentlemen were wearing last evening."

"I thought it might be wise to make a few purchases while I'm in Town, as it could be a long time before I return," the earl said as he straightened his neckcloth. He seemed to be forever fussing with it.

"Don't make it ten years the next time, Ben." Elinor's face was serious as she looked up at her brother.

"Perhaps the next time we see each other, you shall visit my new bride and me in Dorsetshire. It has been a long time since you've been home, Ellie, for which I blame myself. I would be honored if you and your family would come for a long visit."

Cassandra wondered whether Ben's definition of "family" included her. She rather suspected that it didn't, but she did not care. Nothing would appeal to her less than an extended stay in some provincial backwater.

The gentlemen said their farewells and left. Lord Winchfield, Cassandra noted, did not look her in the eye.

When the door had closed behind them, Ellie picked up her teacup and turned to face Cassandra.

"Those two seem to have come to some sort of truce, thank heaven," she said, nodding toward the door.

"Yes." Cassandra admired her brother's strength of character in carrying out Elinor's wishes, and hoped her sister-in-law would not ask about her success in the same endeavor. Fortunately, Elinor chose to focus on more mundane matters.

"What on earth are you doing awake at this hour? I don't think I've ever seen you at breakfast before eleven."

"I could not sleep."

"I'm sorry to hear it. Is anything troubling you?" Elinor's face was all kindness.

Normally, Cassandra would use just such an opening to pour out her heart to her friend. But how could she complain about Lord Winchfield to his own sister? Elinor would be caught between the two, and that would not be fair.

"I suppose I was just overstimulated by the excitement of the evening." Well, that was a partial truth.

To her relief, Elinor accepted that explanation at face value. "That is natural enough. I had trouble sleeping myself for a little while. I have no idea why I awakened so early this morning, but breakfast smelled so good that I could not get back to sleep." Elinor stood to fill her plate at the sideboard. When her back was to Cassandra, she asked, "Did you enjoy your dance with Ben? I hope he didn't tread on your toes."

Her question brought back the whole distressing episode. As Cassandra was trying to phrase a truthful yet diplomatic response, her sister-in-law turned toward her.

"Why the frown, dear? Was the dance so unpleasant?"

"Do you think I'm too cutting, Elinor?" Cassandra blinked at her own question. She had been trying hard not to criticize the earl to his sister, but this was not the question she had meant to ask at all—even though it had bedeviled her throughout the night.

Elinor's eyebrows rose. "Not at all, my dear. You are very loyal, in fact. And if you sometimes make a witty remark about another, out of their hearing, whom does it harm?" She returned to the table, put down her plate, and retook her seat. "Why do you ask?"

Cassandra stirred her cold tea for a moment before

replying. There was nothing for it but to tell the truth. "Your brother told me I was too prone to criticize."

Elinor laughed. "Ben has always been such an upright sort, but he has no concept of Town ways. He has not yet learned that most conversational sallies in London society have no more weight or permanence than snowflakes. Like snowflakes, they are meant simply to be admired for their elegance before they fade away. Poor Ben takes things so much to heart. He likely would have said the same to any London lady. Don't give it a second thought, my dear."

Cassandra wanted very much to believe what Elinor said was true. But some tiny part of her suspected that Lord Winchfield's assessment of her had been justified. She reviewed the conversations she had had last night and was startled to realize how many of them involved poking fun at others. But as Ellie said, if the others never heard, what was the harm? Without a bit of laughter, life in London would lose a lot of its luster.

"Shall we go to Madame Saulnier's today to see about the gown you've ordered for Lady Farnham's ball? I believe you said it would be ready for a fitting today."

"Yes, it will." Cassandra tried to summon up some enthusiasm for the task. "I'm so pleased I went with the watered silk rather than the plain. Since the design itself is rather simple, I think the more exotic fabric will be the making of the gown."

Elinor nodded. "You're right. You have such a good sense about these things. Oh, and I meant to tell you—I asked Richard and Ben to meet us at Gunther's after their foray to Tattersall's. Ben has never had an ice—can you imagine?"

Cassandra couldn't.

As they continued to chat about the dress and their other plans for the day, Cassandra felt her self-composure returning. These were the sorts of things she loved to discuss, which had always given her pleasure. It was only the arrival of Lord Winchfield, with his country ideas of propriety, that had momentarily cast her loose from her moorings.

She must reapply herself to the task of finding him a suitable lady. It would cheer Elinor to see her trying to get along with the earl. It might raise his estimation of Cassandra. And, most importantly, it would hasten his departure from London. Without his censorious eye observing her behavior, she could return to her accustomed ways and stop questioning every word that fell from her lips.

Later that day, after a moderately entertaining day of shopping, the two sets of siblings met for ices at Gunther's. The day had turned surprisingly warm, with the result that quite a crush had developed inside the popular shop. Richard and Lord Winchfield volunteered to wait in the queue while the ladies relaxed in the Blythes' barouche.

"Lord Winchfield," Cassandra whispered, managing to catch the earl's attention while her brother and Elinor were discussing which sweets they should buy.

"Yes?" The earl's manner was all that was polite, but his eyes were cold. Cassandra suddenly understood what Elinor had meant about always having to make the first move where Lord Winchfield was concerned. The gentleman suffered from no shortage of pride.

She took a deep breath. The last thing she wanted

was for Elinor to overhear this conversation and start asking questions, now or later. So she had to speak quickly. "I wish to apologize for my appalling rudeness last evening."

He was silent for about ten seconds or so. She wondered whether he would have the gall to reject her sincere words. But then, to her astonishment, he shook his head and smiled. "No, Lady Cassandra, it is I who must apologize. Or perhaps we are both at fault. What I mean to say is that I spoke too harshly, and I have been trying to find an appropriate moment to apologize ever since sometime this morning, when I finally stopped nursing my grudge and realized what a gudgeon I'd been."

Cassandra blinked. She could not imagine any other gentleman of her acquaintance making such a pretty speech to so bluntly accept the blame for an incident. Perhaps he had realized that his longstanding pique with Elinor and Richard had been a mistake, and decided to be less proud in the future.

Whatever the reason for his quick change of heart, she was glad. It would have been most awkward living under the same roof with the earl for the duration of his visit and barely being on speaking terms. She would have had to explain to Elinor the reasons for her coolness, and that would not have been pleasant.

"Please do not berate yourself. I believe you are correct—we are both at fault in the affair. I would be most pleased if we could forgive each other for the transgression and start afresh."

He grinned, and she was so taken aback that she almost fell out of the barouche. It was only when he smiled that she realized how serious he was most of the time. He had a most appealing smile. If he wished to attract the attention of a lady, all he needed to do was wield that grin. Why, the man even had dimples! He would devastate half of London's drawing rooms if he would just relax a little.

"I agree most heartily with that idea, Lady Cassandra, and tender my forgiveness to you."

"And I to you."

"Are you two going to chat all day, or shall we go collect these demmed ices?" Richard demanded.

"I am at your service, Blythe." Sketching a tiny bow and favoring her with one last smile, Lord Winchfield departed.

"What were you and Ben chattering about?" Elinor asked.

"Nothing, really. Just reviewing some of the events from last night's rout." That was not a lie at all. It just wasn't the entire truth.

"Speaking of the rout—I heard the most amazing bit of news from Mrs. Carroll, and I completely forgot to tell you about it. Did you know that her daughter has caught the eye of an exiled French count?"

"How exotic!"

They were still trading *on-dits* a few minutes later when Elinor stopped in midtale to look behind Cassandra. "Why, Mrs. Lewis, Miss Lewis! What a pleasure to see you!" she exclaimed.

London was really just an overgrown village, Cassandra reflected as Mrs. Lewis and her tongue-tied daughter approached them on foot. Already this afternoon they had run into a dozen acquaintances. The nice weather always seemed to draw everyone to the shops.

"Good afternoon, Lady Elinor, Lady Cassandra."

Mrs. Lewis looked up into the carriage. "It is a fine day to be about in the sunshine, is it not?"

"Indeed it is," Elinor replied.

As they exchanged pleasantries, a thought hit Cassandra. Perhaps with her mother, Cassandra, and Elinor around to provide gentle support, Miss Lewis might be less tongue-tied around the earl than she'd been on their first meeting. Cassandra could not shake the notion that the two quiet, country-loving people would be perfect for each other, if Miss Lewis could be persuaded to talk.

"Will you not join us for a moment or two?" Cassandra opened the carriage door and slid sideways on her bench. Mrs. Lewis readily agreed and clambered inside, but her daughter hesitated.

"Are you waiting for someone?" she asked, glancing about. "I should not like to intrude."

"Our brothers are inside buying ices, but judging from the crowd they shall be a few minutes yet," Cassandra reassured her, patting the seat beside her. With one more glance at the shop, Miss Lewis joined them in the carriage.

She was a graceful little thing, Cassandra noted. With just a bit of encouragement, she might just make an excellent match for the earl. If she did, Cassandra could register several good deeds with one stroke. She would solve the earl's problem, help Miss Lewis escape the city she so despised, *and* fulfill her promise to her mother to be kind to the younger woman.

That would show Lord Winchfield that she was more than a sharp-tongued harridan! But how could she accomplish it? She could not simply wave a wand and endow Miss Lewis with social courage.

To her relief, Miss Lewis did indeed seem more relaxed in the familiar company of her mother and Elinor than she had the other day at the library. She even volunteered several bits of information without being asked, and kept her gaze on her companions for most of the conversation.

Thinking again of the library, Cassandra permitted herself a secret smile. Miss Lewis was well read, and that might serve her well were she to become betrothed to Lord Winchfield. He was also a bookish sort, and perhaps, in time, they could while away the winter hours in the country, talking of authors. This plan seemed more appealing by the minute.

"Ho, wasn't I right, Winchfield?" she heard her brother's jovial voice across the pavement. "I told him I was certain you would have collected several friends by now and that we would be wise to buy extra ices. I am glad you are here, ladies, as we have far more than we could possibly eat ourselves." He distributed ices to Mrs. Lewis and her daughter, while Lord Winchfield handed the treats he carried to Elinor and Cassandra.

When the earl's hand brushed hers, Cassandra was reminded briefly of their dance the other night. Until it had degenerated into an exchange of harsh words, the waltz had been much more enjoyable than she had anticipated it would be. The earl was by no means the best dancer she had ever partnered. Despite that, she had felt more comfortable—more right—in his arms than she had in the embrace of more skilled gentlemen. Even his hand had seemed to fit around hers particularly well. And he hadn't clenched her waist in a viselike grip, as so many men did.

It had been a very odd encounter, from beginning to end. But that was neither here nor there. Cassandra returned her thoughts to the present, where Mrs.

Lewis was arguing with Richard and Lord Winchfield.

"Really, Anne and I should take our leave. We are occupying your seats."

"Please do not disturb yourselves," the earl protested. "I shouldn't think of making a lady give up her seat to me."

"Thank you, my lord," Miss Lewis said with a shy smile. Inwardly, Cassandra rejoiced. It appeared that her friend was actually interested in Lord Winchfield. All the better! It was time to move things along.

"I was thinking," Cassandra announced to no one in particular, "that it might be fun to plan a picnic for early next week, considering how nice the weather is."

"A picnic! What an excellent idea," Elinor exclaimed.

"Would you both be interested in such an excursion?" Cassandra asked Mrs. Lewis. "I was thinking that Richmond might be nice."

The older lady looked at her daughter. "That would be lovely, wouldn't it, Anne?"

Anne looked uncertain as to whether it would be lovely or not, but she clearly did not want to disagree with her parent. She nodded. "I should enjoy that above all things."

"As should I," said Lord Winchfield with a warm smile at Miss Lewis.

Good. Very, very good.

Cassandra glanced at Elinor to see if she had observed the little exchange of looks between her brother and Miss Lewis. To her surprise, she noted an expression of slight but unmistakable displeasure on her sister-in-law's face. Surely she could not dislike a potential liaison between her brother and Miss

Lewis? They were most admirably suited. Cassandra resolved to ask Elinor about it later, when they returned home.

"Then it is settled," Cassandra said, glancing at the assembled company. "Miss Lewis, you should know that Lord Winchfield is an expert on nature. Perhaps while we are in Richmond, he will be able to tell us something about the plants and animals there."

"I would hardly call myself an expert—" the earl began to protest.

"You are certainly more knowledgeable than I and, I wager, most of the rest of us. I know that there are deer in the park at Richmond, as well as all sorts of waterfowl on the river. I will be very interested to learn anything new about them that I can."

There. That seems suitably positive. No one could say she wasn't trying her best to build up Lord Winchfield's character in Miss Lewis's eyes. And judging from the look of interest on the younger woman's face, her efforts seemed to be bearing fruit.

She hazarded a glance at Lord Winchfield and was surprised to see him looking at her with raised eyebrows. It was clear that he knew exactly what she was trying to accomplish.

It didn't matter. In fact, that was all to the good. Let him see that she had a selfless side, too. Perhaps it would improve his opinion of her.

Miss Lewis, fortunately, seemed oblivious to any efforts being made on her behalf. In a small voice, she asked the earl what sorts of animals he studied back in Dorsetshire, and the two began a quiet conversation.

Cassandra sat back against the squabs and ate her ice with satisfaction. If the fates were smiling on her, she would have succeeeded in engineering an alliance between Lord Winchfield and Miss Lewis within the month.

She hesitated in her determined attack on the icy treat as the word "engineering" occurred to her. Had she not accused the earl of trying to do the very same thing to his sister?

That had been different, she told herself. He had tried to force his sister to marry Lord Penwood. She wasn't trying to force anyone to do anything. She was just planting a few useful ideas in their heads and sitting back to watch them grow.

CHAPTER SIX

"What can Cassandra be thinking, to be trying to push Ben together with Miss Lewis?" Elinor knew she sounded pettish, but she could not help it.

"I'm sure I don't know. For once, she's actually trying to be helpful. Very odd."

Richard's gentle mockery usually made Elinor laugh, but not today. The stakes for this picnic were too high.

She looked out the window at the pretty landscape that had begun unfolding before them several minutes previously, when they had finally left the urban edges of London behind. The new shoots in the fields were brilliantly green in the late spring sunshine. It was a perfect day for being in the country, and her heart should have been light.

But it wasn't. Despite Richard's doubts, she was certain that Cassandra and Ben would be ideally matched. Her frustration at her inability to convince everyone else—including the two people involved—of the wisdom of this plan was beginning to wear her down.

She felt a small tug on her skirt. "Mama, how much further is it to Richmond?"

She smiled at her four-year-old daughter. She was glad that she had decided to have the children ride with her and not with their nurse, ensconced in the

Blythes' small gig. "Not far now, sweeting. And when we get there, there will be cake."

Alice clapped her hands. "And lemonade?"

"Yes."

"And ducks?" piped up six-year-old David.

"I'll do my best."

The children traded looks of intense excitement. Elinor marveled at how easy it was, sometimes, to please children. If only adults were so simple.

She glanced out the back of the barouche toward the carriages that followed. One thing had gone as she had hoped: Cassandra was riding with Ben in his carriage. Unfortunately, Mrs. Lewis and her daughter were there as well, and Elinor was certain that Cassandra was doing her best to encourage Ben's slight interest in the girl.

When Elinor had questioned Cassandra's plan the previous afternoon, her sister-in-law had laughed off her concerns. "Really, Ellie, it's a perfect solution," she'd said. "Miss Lewis shall have her quiet country life and Lord Winchfield shall have his biddable, pliant wife." Without the ability to suggest a substitute plan—for she could not inform Cassandra of her hopes for a liaison between her and Ben, for fear of being laughed out of the room—she had had no luck changing Cassandra's mind on the issue.

They had already disagreed about the guest list for the picnic. Elinor had thought that it might be useful to enlarge the size of the party. The presence of more people would give Ben opportunities to speak to someone besides Miss Lewis. And the larger group would likely still the shy woman's tongue even more, revealing to Ben just what a mouse she was.

It wasn't that Elinor disliked Miss Lewis. On the

contrary, she thought she was sweet. She just believed that Miss Lewis was absolutely wrong for Ben, and Ben for her. The two of them would scamper back to Dorsetshire and molder away like genteel octogenarians, and that wouldn't be good for either of them.

So Elinor had invited a few more people to join the party. To Cassandra's delight, she'd invited Peregrine Russell and Edward Symes. But her sister-in-law had been less enthusiastic about the invitation Elinor had extended to Lady Louisa Dennis and her brother, Viscount Halmond.

"Honestly, Ellie, I do not know what you see in Lady Louisa," Cassandra had grumbled as they'd sat in Elinor's private sitting room sipping chocolate. "She is boorish and loud, and makes no pretense of the fact that she is a fortune hunter."

"The woman can't help the fact that Halmond lost a bit of money at cards," she'd responded mildly.

"A bit of money! He lost their *house*."

Elinor had been forced to concede that that particular wager had been a bit unwise.

"And he does nothing to stop his own sister from throwing herself at every eligible bachelor in London. It's unpleasant to watch, to say the least." Cassandra's face had worn the mulish expression Elinor knew so well, having seen it often on her husband's face. The Blythes were nothing if not stubborn.

"I feel sorry for Lady Louisa, but she does not seem to mind terribly. I know she is eager to marry, so the fact that she must marry a fortune is just a small complication."

"Would you mind if she set her cap for your brother?"

Elinor had paused at that thought. "Well, I'm not

sure. I don't think she would be the type Ben would fancy. She's rather loud, as you have mentioned."

"It might not matter whether he fancies her or not. I have heard several dark *on-dits* around Town intimating that her family's financial troubles have grown dire. I would not put it past her to try to trick some eligible gentleman into a betrothal."

"That's a terrible thing to say about any lady!"

Cassandra had shrugged. "I know it will go no further. I just thought it prudent to warn you."

"I think you're being overly cautious. I have known Lady Louisa and her brother for years. In any case, I can hardly withdraw the invitation."

"That's true." Cassandra had lapsed into a disgruntled silence.

Looking back at the small procession of carriages now, Elinor noted with unease that Lady Louisa and her brother had arranged to ride to Richmond in Mr. Russell's carriage. Viscount Halmond had said his vehicle was being repaired, but Elinor had heard it whispered that he'd had to sell it to pay his debts. Could things be as terrible for the siblings as Cassandra had hinted? And would Lady Louisa be driven to desperate straits?

"Mama, will there be rabbits in Richmond?" David's eager voice interrupted her musings. She twisted around.

"I suspect there will," she told her son, as she wrested her mind away from unpleasant thoughts and turned it toward amusing the children for the last few miles of the trip.

* * *

"Are you fond of bird watching, Miss Lewis?" Cassandra asked brightly.

The younger girl nodded. "There are lots of birds to see at home in Lincolnshire. Surely you must remember, Lady Cassandra?"

To be honest, she did not. Sometimes she quite forgot that she had spent most of the first seventeen years of her life in Lincolnshire. The Seasons her family had spent in London loomed large in her recollections, while the longer portion of the year they had spent in the country had shrunk in her mind until her main memories were of card parties, Christmas dinners, assemblies, and so forth. Aside from riding, she had always been one to spend much of her life indoors. Picnics were about as close as she liked to get to the natural world. "Of course," she answered Miss Lewis's query about birds vaguely.

"I have heard that the Humber estuary is an excellent place to spot birds of all sorts," Lord Winchfield chimed in.

"Yes, indeed it is! I once saw a great gray shrike there, and a gull-billed tern on another occasion."

Cassandra leaned back against the tufted carriage seat and turned her attention to Mrs. Lewis, relieved that she had finally set a conversational fire under Miss Lewis and Lord Winchfield. They had so much in common that she found it amazing they could find so little about which to converse without her help. That would change, though, she felt confident. It was like starting a fire in a grate. Once a few small coals were burning, the rest would catch soon enough.

"It was very kind of you to invite us to join this picnic," Mrs. Lewis remarked. "It is good for Anne to get out of the city once in a while."

They chatted about inconsequential things for the remainder of the journey to Richmond. Once John Coachman had spotted a suitable place for them to arrange their picnic things, everyone alighted from the carriages and strolled toward the flat, grassy spot by the edge of the river.

"This is perfect!" Lady Louisa exclaimed in her braying voice. "I am so glad you invited us on this picnic, Lady Elinor."

Cassandra repressed the thought that at least someone was glad that Lady Louisa and her brother had been invited. She was trying very hard to be more generous about other people, particularly those she did not like. Lord Winchfield's comments from the night of the rout still rankled. Ever since he had complained of her critical nature, she had listened to herself and had been rather shocked at the invective that casually streamed from her lips at the slightest provocation. It was a bad habit she had developed without even noticing it, rather like chewing one's fingernails. Wit was one thing, but misanthropy was quite another.

"This picnic will keep Lady Louisa off the streets of London for today, at least," Perry Russell whispered in Cassandra's ear. "For that, I think the gentlemen of White's owe your sister-in-law a round. Too bad she can't collect."

"Shhh, Perry. Don't be cruel—it doesn't suit you," Cassandra muttered.

"Of course it does. It's my *raison d'être*. Don't worry. Lady Louisa can't possibly have heard."

"All the same . . ." Cassandra let her voice trail away, uncertain how to make her point without coming off as a prig.

"Don't tell me you're becoming provincial, my dear," Perry said in a reproving voice.

"No. Perhaps I'm just getting a little tired of the endless points scored at others' expense."

Perry let out a low, toneless whistle. "Well, to paraphrase Mr. Johnson, when one is tired of wit, one is tired of life—and definitely tired of London."

"I wouldn't go that far," she said as she reached the spot where several footmen were laying out thick blankets. From the corner of her eye, she saw her niece and nephew sprinting toward a small rabbit in the grass. The bunny immediately bounded far from their reach, and they shrieked with delight as it disappeared over a hillock.

Mr. Russell followed her eye. "Charming children."

"I think so." She beamed.

"I was being facetious." He laughed. "You know that children terrify me."

"Don't be silly. You were one once."

"I also used to live in Yorkshire. Don't damn me for past sins."

"Yorkshire! At least I had the decency to grow up in the Home Counties." Edward Symes had joined them. "I don't believe I ever knew you were from Yorkshire, Russell. How on earth did you manage to eradicate that grating accent?"

"A great deal of money spent with a very good elocution teacher can work wonders."

The talk shifted toward their years at Oxford, as it often did, and Cassandra drifted away to stand by a tree and watch Alice and David as they continued to chase rabbits, sparrows, and just about anything else in the park that was smaller and faster than they. After luncheon, she decided, she would join them in their games.

She often wished she spent more time in the children's company. They were most amiable companions. Of course, that was easy for her to say, as she had no hand at all in their upbringing. She could simply act the part of the indulgent aunt, rewarding them with sweets or toys whenever the fancy struck her. It would be a completely different situation once she had children of her own.

If that day ever came. As the Season wore on, Cassandra found herself wondering, as she had last year, whether she had waited too long and played her cards too close to her chest. At four-and-twenty, she was dangerously close to being on the shelf; she knew there were some who said she was there already. Certainly, she still had a reputation as an Incomparable, but society was fickle and time would do its work. Already, she had made the acquaintance of most of the society gentleman who frequented London during the Season. Not one of them had appeared to be the sort of gentleman she could bear gazing at over scones and preserves every morning *and* envision as the father of her children. The witty men did not seem husbandly. And the husbandly ones were, in general, not at all witty.

It was a dilemma. Perhaps it would be wisest to simply get used to the idea that she might never find a congenial husband, and to start making plans for other ways to fill her days. Perhaps, if she could interest a theater manager in one of her plays—

"Lost in thought, Lady Cassandra?" came a low, familiar voice that was neither husbandly nor witty—simply polite.

She looked up into Lord Winchfield's face. He was standing just behind her, observing the children as they ran about under their nurse's supervision.

"Just watching Alice and David. They seem to be having so much fun. Life used to be much less complicated," she said absently.

"Unfortunately we grow up and take on responsibilities—earldoms, estates, tenants, and all sorts of other things we could not even visualize at that age." An odd note in his voice caught her attention. He sounded almost wistful.

"Am I to infer from that that you would much rather have remained a child?" she asked with a smile.

"Not a child, no. But there are days when I wonder whether being an earl was the best hand to have been dealt."

"I'm sure it must be difficult. All those riches to count, all that land to look at, all those neighbors to impress." After speaking, she had a moment of dismay. She had meant her words as a joke, but would the earl take them that way?

Fortunately, a glimmer of that grin that had so fascinated her the other day outside Gunther's flickered across his face. "*Touché,* Lady Cassandra. You are right. I am so much more fortunate than most, and I do realize it. I did not mean to complain about my lot, which is a most comfortable one. It is just that, sometimes, I wonder whether the earldom would have been better served with another heir."

"Another heir?"

"Ellie and I had an older brother, who died as an infant. I sometimes imagine how my life would have differed, had he lived."

"And what do you envision?" A peer who did not

relish his powers and perquisites was a creature outside her experience, and she truly wanted to know.

Lord Winchfield crossed his arms and leaned against the small beech tree beneath which they stood, flattening his fine new coat against the dusty bark. He must be the horror of his valet, she thought with an inward chuckle.

"I like to think my older brother would have let me skulk about the place unmolested, studying my ants and sketching my small mammals. In my imaginings, he is a grand sort of gentleman who would enjoy all the deference and pageantry that comes with the title, and who would not have felt overwhelmed by the responsibilities."

"Is that how you feel? Overwhelmed?"

"Not exactly. Almost nothing has occurred in the decade I have held the title that I have not felt able to address." He paused. "I suppose that sounds rather self-satisfied."

"Not at all. I asked you a direct question and you answered it honestly."

He nodded. "Probably the only time I felt out of my depth was during Elinor's elopement. I had no idea how to convince her of the wisdom of my approach—" He held up a hand. "But we have already discussed this, and I don't wish to incur your wrath once more. It is much more pleasant to be your friend than your enemy."

She smiled. "I agree. So aside from that episode, it isn't lack of ability to manage the estate that has distressed you."

"No. It is merely that I don't feel like much of a peer. In my heart, I'm a scientist. The role my title confers on me sometimes feels like a set of unfamiliar clothes I am forced by circumstance to wear."

His confession startled Cassandra. She had felt the same way herself, although she had never tried to put it into words so precisely. The sentiment often overcame her when she heard someone toasting her health at a party. She remembered feeling it deeply when a suitor—whom she later dismissed with as much kindness as possible—wrote a poem in her honor. She remembered little of the ode now, so embarrassed had she been, but it had included something about flaxen hair and eyes the color of a summer sky. She shuddered. She knew exactly what Lord Winchfield meant about playing a part for which one felt ill accustomed.

"Are you all right, Lady Cassandra?" His brow was furrowed. "You have the most peculiar expression on your face."

"Do I?" She laughed. "I was just thinking that I understand your sentiments. When gentlemen laud me as an Incomparable, I want to protest that I'm merely an ordinary person whom fate has favored with a pretty face. That makes me no different from anyone else, underneath."

He laughed. "We all differ from each other, both underneath and on the surface. If we did not, life would be boring indeed." Before he could add anything to this intriguing thought, a loud shout to their left claimed their attention.

"Oh heavens, oh heavens!" came a woman's anguished cry. "Dear God!"

Cassandra swiveled her head in search of the source of the sound, and soon found it. The children's nurse was standing as still as stone, gazing in horror

toward the shoreline of the river, with six-year-old
David at her feet.

Where was Alice? With icy dread, Cassandra saw a
small billow of yellow at the water's edge.

CHAPTER SEVEN

"Lord Winchfield—" Cassandra began as she started to run toward the shore. But she was speaking to empty air. The earl was already a good distance away, sprinting toward the river with loping strides. She raced behind him, heedless of the rocks and tree roots that threatened to topple her.

Nothing could have happened to Alice in such a short time, she reassured herself as she ran, her breath heaving in and out of her lungs in increasingly harsh gasps. *All of us were here. She couldn't have been in the water for more than a second or two. She will be all right.*

From her right she saw Richard and Elinor making haste toward the river as well. Surely one of them would reach the river before—well, before the unthinkable.

No sooner had she had that thought than she saw the earl shrug out of his jacket and toss it on the ground. Moments later, a splash echoed from the shore, as Lord Winchfield strode into the undoubtedly icy river. It appeared to be shallow at that point; the water barely reached his knees. Within moments, he had reached the little yellow bundle and scooped it up in his arms.

Cassandra held her breath.

The bundle began to move. Small feet kicked out from under the yellow skirt, and Cassandra heard a faint, sputtering cough.

Thank God.

As though moving of their own volition without her conscious thought, her feet soon brought her to the river's edge. Lord Winchfield had almost reached the grassy edge with his precious armload. Once he was back on dry land, he picked up his jacket and put it around the wet child.

"Alice!" Elinor's voice was weak with relief as she hurried toward her daughter. That tone changed almost instantly to anger. "You are a very, very naughty little girl. Hasn't Nurse told you not to go near the water?"

Still in her uncle's arms, Alice nodded, then shivered.

"I have, my lady. I tell her every day." The nurse had finally reached them, a bewildered David at her side. She was gasping. "Young Master David had fallen and skinned his knee. I was tending to it and I was certain that Miss Alice was right behind me. David was struggling against the liniment and I was trying to soothe him—I am so sorry, my lady." She struggled for breath, and Cassandra's heart went out to her. She had always found the nurse to be a kind and conscientious woman, devoted to the welfare of her two tiny charges. This was a dreadful mistake that could have happened to anyone.

"It is all right, Nurse," Richard said in a clipped voice. "We shall figure out later what happened when." He turned his attention to Alice, and gently lifted the child from Lord Winchfield's arms. "Did you bring a change of clothing for her?" he asked the nurse.

"Yes, my lord. I shall fetch it immediately." Probably grateful to be given something concrete to do, the nurse hurried away toward the carriages.

Richard looked down at Alice. "You are in a great deal of trouble, Alice," he said in a stern voice.

She looked up at him, her lower lip trembling. "But I saw a duck."

"It does not matter. You know you're not supposed to go near the water."

"I know. But it was a *baby* duck," she said, her eyes wide, as though it should be patently obvious that this fact would override any previous parental dictates.

Cassandra saw the corner of her brother's mouth quiver in a way she knew well. Richard could play the disciplinarian when required, but in truth his children both had him wound around their pudgy fingers.

All of us play roles in which, to some extent, we are frauds, she thought, recalling the conversation she had been having with Lord Winchfield just before Alice's fall.

That gentleman now stood a few yards from the excited knot of people on the shore, breathing heavily. His neckcloth was askew, his hair ruffled, and his face damp with sweat, but no polished gentleman in a London drawing room had ever looked half so attractive to Cassandra.

She strolled toward him. "Thank you, my lord," she murmured. "I know Ellie and Richard will thank you, too, once they have recovered from the shock."

He shook his head. "No thanks are needed. I did what anyone would have done. I simply reached her first."

"That alone took presence of mind. It seems poor Nurse was rooted to the spot in shock. And by the time I had figured out what was happening, you were already halfway to the river."

"The important thing is that we saw her. I don't think she had had her head below the water for more than a few seconds. She told me that she reached out to pet a duckling and lost her balance."

Cassandra grinned, almost giddy with relief now that the fright was past. "That sounds like Alice. She and David both adore animals. It must be a Rowland family trait."

He smiled, and her breath caught in a peculiar way in her throat. The snowy whiteness of his shirt seemed to accentuate the healthy glow of his face and the long column of his throat, which was clearly visible now that his neckcloth was in twisted ruins. She was suddenly aware of the broad line of his shoulders, which was much more visible now than it had been in his blue superfine coat. Much more aware was she, too, of the length of his legs, accentuated by the wet pantaloons that clung to his calves even more tightly than before.

He might be a quiet country scholar, but at the moment he did not exactly look the part. Cassandra felt a dull flush staining her cheeks.

How could she be thinking such . . . improper . . . thoughts about stuffy Lord Winchfield? He was arrogant, and priggish, and provincial. . . .

"You appear distracted, Lady Cassandra." His voice held an undercurrent of laughter. She looked into his eyes—and realized, without a doubt, that he knew exactly what she had been thinking. Her cheeks grew even warmer. What must he think of her? What did she think of herself?

For a moment they simply stared at each other,

their eyes communicating far more than words ever could. Why had she never before noticed the startling color of his eyes? They were some undefined blend of hazel and emerald.

A thread of something rich and warm seemed to hang between them. She was afraid to speak, for fear that it would snap.

"Lady Cassandra," he said in a low, hesitant voice, as though he, too, sensed their odd connection, "I—"

"Your new coat appears to be much the worse for wear, Winchfield," Richard said with a rueful chuckle as he approached them, Alice still in his arms. "I shall have it cleaned and repaired for you, of course. And I cannot thank you enough for rescuing Alice. I will always be deeply in your debt."

"Don't worry in the slightest about the coat. I do not. And as for coming to Alice's assistance, it was the least I could do as her doting uncle," the earl replied. "Perhaps, in some small way, this day will make up for the grief I caused you and Elinor so long ago."

"Not only does it make up for that entirely, it supercedes it. And you were not wholly at fault in the matter of our elopement, you know. If I had not been so impatient, things might not have happened as they did." He sighed. "I acted like what I was—a rash and bullheaded adolescent. I would also like to tender my apologies for absconding with your sister."

"And I accept. Let us speak no more of that episode, and consider it well and truly past."

Richard nodded. "Nothing would give me greater pleasure."

Awkwardly, as Richard struggled to balance Alice on one arm, the two men shook hands on the resolution.

Cassandra looked on with a small smile. Her

brother and the earl were men of character—ready for any challenge and unafraid to admit their mistakes. It was surprising how few gentlemen of the *ton* fit that description.

At a distance, she saw Elinor, Nurse, and David approaching, the children's caretaker carrying a small satchel. When they arrived, Elinor extracted her daughter from her husband's arms.

"We have a new dress here for Alice. Once she is changed, I think we should return to London. I don't want her to get a chill."

This was the first thing anyone had said in the last few minutes that had caught Alice's attention. "Noooooo!" the child wailed.

"But, Alice—" her mother began.

"Noooooooooo! Want to stay heeeeeeeere!"

At Elinor's feet, David took up the cry. "Don't want to go hooooome!"

"Children!" Richard's voice was sharp. "Stop this nonsense."

"Noooooooooo!" both children howled. "Want to stay heeeeeeeere!"

Richard shot Cassandra a look of pure frustration. She found it amusing to see her confident brother brought to heel by two small children.

It was the earl, surprisingly, who brought order to the rapidly devolving scene. "Are there extra blankets to be had?"

Elinor nodded. "I don't know what the footmen were thinking. They brought enough for twice the number of people."

"Good. Once Alice is changed and dry, we can wrap her in a few blankets and settle down with her in the sun. She will be just as warm, or warmer, than she would be in her own bed in London, without the delay of the journey home."

Elinor looked skeptical. "But she shouldn't be rewarded after disobeying."

Lord Winchfield shook his head. "She won't be." He held out his arms for his niece, and Elinor handed her over. The child had not touched the ground since the earl had fished her out of the river.

Making sure his coat was still wrapped snugly around Alice, the earl held her high above his head. "Are you sorry for frightening us all to death?"

She nodded, giggling as he swung her slightly back and forth.

"And will you sit still for the rest of the picnic, and stay close to Nurse or your parents?"

"But what if there is a rabbit? Or a duck?"

"You will have to watch it from a distance."

She kicked her feet beneath his long coat. "Noooooo . . ."

He gave her a tiny toss in the air. "If you are good, and do as I say, at the end of the day I will hold you up like this again, and spin you around a few times for good measure."

She stuck a finger in her bow-shaped mouth and regarded him. "Can I look for birds too?"

He shook his head. "When you disobeyed Nurse, you lost the right to look for birds. When you make choices, you have to live with the consequences."

"What is 'quences'?"

"Um . . ."

"Results," Cassandra chimed in. "What happens as a result of what you've done."

The little girl was silent. It wasn't clear whether she

understood or not, but at least she wasn't protesting anymore.

"Do we agree?" her uncle asked, lowering her toward the ground.

Her face mutinous, she nodded.

"Good." He set her on the grass, where Nurse immediately took her hand and led her toward a small copse of trees so that she could dry and change the child.

"I'd never believe you had no children of your own, Ben," his sister said with a laugh as she watched them go. "Where did you learn to reason like that?"

He shrugged. "No idea. Maybe from watching the grooms at Winchfield Hall wheedle deals from you when we were children. You and Alice are a lot alike."

"Oh, really?"

"Yes. Let me see." He ticked off points on his fingers. "You don't listen to authority. You like to run away . . ."

"Very funny." Elinor slapped him playfully on the arm. "Well, I don't care how you did it, but thank you"—she paused—"for everything." Her voice caught on that last word and a tear spilled down her cheek. "Why should I be crying now?" she asked no one in particular, as more tears followed the first.

"The crisis is over, and you are just realizing now what might have happened." Her husband gathered his wife into his arms and rocked her. "Shhh, Elinor. It is all over, and no one was harmed."

After a moment, she pulled away and wiped her eyes with a rueful smile. "Thank you. I promise to control myself. We should return to our guests."

With one last round of thanks to Lord Winchfield, Richard and Ellie departed, Richard's arm about his wife's shoulders. As Cassandra and the earl stood watching them in silence, the strange gossamer thread seemed to wind itself between them again. But Cassandra knew that she couldn't allow it to weave its magic once more.

She had simply been addled by the earl's disheveled appearance, by his heroism—by the fresh air and sunshine, for all she knew. She could not possibly be attracted to stodgy Lord Winchfield, and she had to quickly dissuade him from any thought that she was. The last thing she needed was another unwanted, love-struck swain dogging her footsteps this Season. She hoped to convince Perry of her worthiness before the summer was out, and she didn't want any distractions.

"Your pantaloons are sopping, my lord, and I doubt that Nurse has brought a spare pair for you," she said with a grin. "Shall I fetch you one of the extra blankets so that you might dry yourself?"

He looked at her for a long moment, then shook his head. "No, thank you. I believe Tyson left one of my small traveling cases in the carriage—we've each been meaning to remove it ever since I arrived in London. I am certain there is at least a towel in there." With that, he turned and walked away toward the carriages.

Cassandra watched him for a moment or two. Stuffy he might be, but he certainly cut a fine figure.

Don't be foolish, she admonished herself. *What use would you have for the Earl of Winchfield, and what use would he have for you?*

Two hours later, everyone was dry and the trauma of the morning had been largely forgotten. All the guests had praised Cook's picnic. Many of the adults, except for Mrs. Lewis and her daughter, had imbibed a fair quantity of ratafia or claret, and as a result they were feeling most charitable toward the rest of the party and, indeed, the rest of the world. Cassandra had even quelled her resentment toward Lady Louisa and her brother, who both seemed to be on their best behavior. Lord Halmond had not suggested even so much as a game of cards, making this day something of a watershed for him. By all accounts, he was usually well into deep play at White's, or some less respectable gambling den, by noon.

"I see the hero of the day is still pursuing the voluble Miss Lewis," Perry observed, nodding toward Lord Winchfield and said lady, who were strolling near the water's edge.

"Heaven only knows why," remarked Elinor, frowning as she popped a grape into her mouth.

Cassandra debated arguing in Miss Lewis's favor with her sister-in-law and decided that they had already tilled that ground deeply enough. Elinor believed that her brother and Miss Lewis were too much alike, and that they would soon have little to say to each other. Cassandra did not believe in the old adage that opposites attract, and felt that the couple's similarity would be their strength.

"So have you figured out a way to make the second act of your play more exciting?" Perry asked Cassandra as he leaned back on his elbows and stretched his legs out in front of him. "Any more ideas for expanding the character of Sir Humphrey what's-his-name?"

"Mills. Sir Humphrey Mills."

"Right. Good name. Seems suitably pompous."

"Someone burdened with the Christian name 'Peregrine' should not cast aspersions."

He smiled and flopped further back on the blanket. " 'Tis my cross to bear. I can hardly be blamed for the fact that it was the name of my mother's favorite uncle. But enough about me. How have you altered the character?"

"The problem was that there was no reason for him to act as he did. He was just priggish and moralizing because it suited the action of the play," Cassandra said, leaning forward as she warmed to her subject. "But then it occurred to me that his main motivation could be a need to control his surroundings. All of his life, he's been surrounded by events he could not manipulate. Even now, the other characters in the play give no thought as to how their actions affect him. His constant comments urging people to behave are his way of trying to take charge of things."

Perry exhaled deeply. "Sounds very dour."

"It isn't, really. He is supposed to be the foil for the other witty characters."

"Well, let us speak of them, then. Have you come up with any other delicious lines for Lady Saunderton?"

"A few. Remember the scene in the drawing room, when she learns that her son has made a fool of himself in Hyde Park, chasing after the beautiful Miss Finch?"

"Yes."

"Well, I now have her say, 'A bird in the hand is worth two in the park.' "

Perry clapped his hands. "Marvelous! What else have you come up with?"

She and Perry chatted a few minutes more about the play's *bon mots*—she knew they were the main aspect of the theater that interested him, and that anything about plot or character bored him to distraction. After a few minutes, the earl and Miss Lewis joined them.

"What are you discussing?" the earl asked, holding out his hand to steady his companion as she sat down.

"A play I'm in the midst of writing."

Lord Winchfield stared at her.

"A play!" Miss Lewis breathed. "I did not know you were a playwright, Lady Cassandra."

She laughed, and tried to sound light and carefree. "I'm not sure I can call myself such, since none of my works has been produced. Strangely enough, theater managers and directors are not overly receptive to the scribblings of a mere female, and a flighty society lady at that."

"Female playwrights are rare, are they not?" said the earl, folding his long legs beneath him to join them on the blanket. "I know there are female novelists, such as the author of *Pride and Prejudice,* but even she styles herself as simply 'A Lady.' And it seems to be that the theater is even more outré than the world of publishing."

Cassandra shrugged, even though his disdain hurt. "Perhaps the low regard in which actresses are held translates to all ladies who dare to associate themselves with the theater."

"That makes sense. I must admit that I was a bit taken aback when you mentioned that you write for the theater. Aren't watercolors and embroidery more common creative outlets for ladies? Even novel writing seems a bit more within the pale than the theater." He scowled.

Cassandra resisted the urge to lash out at the earl

for his superciliousness. After all, the man had been a hero today. It would seem churlish. "I am useless at both painting and sewing. And before you ask, I have no talent at the pianoforte, either." She sighed. "As for writing novels, that has never held much appeal for me. Believe me, I have tried my hand at a novel several times. However, I have no patience with writing long reams of description. I prefer to have the characters moving about and saying things."

"That does not surprise me," said Lord Winchfield, his face unreadable.

"So what is the play you are writing now?" Miss Lewis asked, her eyes wide with interest.

"It is a society satire. It is very light and, I hope, amusing."

"What is the issue that you are satirizing?" Lord Winchfield's voice was neutral, as though he really didn't care about the answer.

"The issue?" What could he mean?

"I probably have this wrong, as I have never had much interest in theater," he continued in that maddeningly superior voice. "But does not a satire usually have a target? For instance, didn't Alexander Pope wish to mock the frivolity of feminine fashion when he wrote *The Rape of the Lock*?"

"Well, yes," she said, biding her time as she figured out how to reply. She had always thought her plays satirized life in general, rather than any particular issue. "I suppose you can say I'm satirizing the foibles of society."

He rested his elbow on his thigh and his chin on his hand. "If you had a narrower target, perhaps it might be easier to write. And then you could include some more serious content to counterbalance the light material."

For someone with no interest in theater, he certainly seemed to have his fair share of opinions about it, Cassandra thought.

"But that's just the point, Winchfield," Perry piped up. "There *is* no serious content. It's supposed to be funny."

"I know, but all humor is based on something serious. If it doesn't have a deeper root, it doesn't make people laugh."

Perry frowned, as though he wished to make a retort about the earl's fitness to comment on matters of comedy, but restrained himself. Perhaps Cassandra's earlier admonitions to be kind had found their mark with her friend after all.

Despite her annoyance with the earl's high-handed dismissal of her interest in theater, she was eager to keep Perry from antagonizing Lord Winchfield. Such a conversation would only distress Elinor.

"That makes good sense," she interjected before Perry could change his mind. "I find that I sometimes get caught up in knots writing funny lines that do not advance the story. They're just there to make people laugh, and after a while it gets monotonous."

The earl leveled a triumphant look at Perry, to Cassandra's surprise. She didn't think Lord Winchfield had a petty bone in his body. It was good to know that Elinor's virtue-touting brother could be just as childish as the rest of the *ton*. It made him more human, somehow.

"Lady Elinor!" she heard Lady Louisa calling from halfway across the meadow. The woman should really wait until she was within speaking range, instead of shouting all over the park like some adolescent hoyden, Cassandra thought. As soon as the observation crossed her mind, she sighed. It seemed that she was incapable of thinking positive thoughts about the red-haired woman, no matter how hard she tried.

"Lady Elinor, this is the most amazing coincidence! A dear friend of mine whom I have not seen in several years just happens to be here on a picnic too," Lady Louisa exclaimed a few moments later as she reached them and came to a stop behind Lord Winchfield. "I would like to introduce you to her, if I may." She nodded to a dark-haired woman behind her, who was dressed in the latest stare of fashion, from her beribboned hat to the silk slippers poking out from beneath her ruffled skirts. The lady seemed familiar to Cassandra. Likely they had attended some society function or other together over the past few years. The *ton* was small, but not small enough that Cassandra could identify all its members by name.

Elinor stood. "Certainly." She smiled at the stranger. "Lady Elinor Blythe, this is Miss Georgina Wells."

Cassandra missed the rest of the introduction, as her attention was captured by Lord Winchfield. A most peculiar expression had appeared on his face, as though he had just swallowed something most distasteful.

"I should also introduce you to the rest of the party," Lady Louisa was saying to her friend. "Lord Winchfield?"

"Oh, that is all right," said Miss Wells in a low, silky voice as the earl came to his feet and extended his hand. "Lord Winchfield and I are old friends."

"Old friends" was putting rather too high a gloss on it, Ben thought with a sour feeling in his stomach as he shook the hand of the woman he'd once hoped to marry—before she'd come very close to making him the laughingstock of Dorsetshire.

Her hand was still as soft and smooth as he remembered, her gray eyes still as sparkling, her skin still as unblemished. It was astonishing, really, how such an unsavory personality could be concealed in such an appealing package.

"It has been a while, Miss Wells," he said, hoping his voice was cool and polite. Inside, he felt anything but that.

"I must confess that I am astonished to see you here in London—well, on the outskirts of London." She laughed that musical laugh that had long ago lost its ability to beguile him. "How on earth did you manage to leave behind your beloved beetles?"

"Ants," he muttered.

"I'm sorry?" She knew very well that she had erred and that he had corrected her. It had always been one of her favorite strategies: to play the innocent. She did it so well she should have been on the stage.

"It is no matter." He took a deep breath. "I came to London to visit my sister, whom you've already met." He nodded toward Elinor.

"And to continue your search for a wife?" Georgina asked, raising her perfectly arched eyebrows. "Have you exhausted the highways and country lanes of Dorsetshire?"

"Not quite. I am sure there are many gentle, well-born ladies in the county. I've just had the bad luck not to meet any." Well, that was a slur on some of the pleasant women he *had* met. But he knew Georgina would take the insult personally. She was the only person on earth who brought out this ugly side of him. He could not seem to stop himself.

Her frown showed that his barb had hit its mark. "Perhaps you just fail to appreciate the ladies of Dorsetshire properly."

"Perhaps." This very public conversation was becoming demmed uncomfortable. He should sit down, but some evil, primal force compelled him to ask one last question. "What brings *you* to the capital, Miss Wells? Last time we spoke, you mentioned a *tendre* for a local gentleman back home. I would have thought you would be deep in the midst of wedding preparations, if not married by now."

That pealing laugh rang out again. "Oh no, not yet, my lord. I have yet to find the gentleman who truly meets all my requirements." She leveled a glance at the rest of the group and her eye settled on Peregrine Russell. "But we are being very rude. You have not introduced me to your friends."

As basic courtesy dictated, he did as she asked, even though he devoutly wished he could stride back to his carriage, set the horses into a good gallop, and put as many miles as possible between himself and the odious Georgina Wells.

Of course he should have expected to see her in London. How stupid not to have prepared himself for that very real possibility. When he'd heard Lady Louisa pronounce her name, he felt as he had when he'd once knocked his head against a low-hanging rafter in the barn at Winchfield Hall.

In a haze, he completed the introductions. He must have been doing a better job than he feared of keeping his disgust in check, because everyone in the little party greeted Georgina with what appeared to be genuine warmth. Everyone, that is, except Lady Cassandra. While her words and demeanor were perfectly polite, an unfamiliar reserve masked her smile, and her eyes were hooded when she traded harmless pleasantries with Georgina. She was obviously the only one who had detected the current of unpleasantness in his conversation with the poised brunette.

To his relief, Georgina did not overstay her welcome. Lady Louisa and Lord Halmond offered to walk her back across the grassy fields to her party, which had spread out its own picnic under the shade of an enormous oak. As the three made their way across the park, Ben noticed that Miss Wells and Lady Louisa seemed deep in conversation, their heads close together. Every so often he could hear Georgina's distinctive laugh. If Lady Louisa considered Georgina such a bosom bow, it was not a mark in her favor.

"A penny for your thoughts?" Lady Cassandra murmured as she sat down beside him.

He shrugged. His history with Georgina was an unpleasant, though far from uncommon, story. "I doubt they'd be worth that much."

"What did she do to you?"

He glanced around at the assembled company. Everyone else appeared absorbed in separate conversations, but he did not want to take the risk of this story being overheard. Yet, suddenly, he wanted to talk about it. He had never told another living soul about it since it had happened, and seeing Georgina today had brought it all back to him in painful detail.

"Would you care to accompany me for a short stroll along the river, Lady Cassandra?" he asked in a voice that would carry at least to Elinor, seated a few feet away with Alice cuddled at her side.

Lady Cassandra smiled. "That would be lovely," she said as she stood.

Once they were out of earshot of the party, she turned to him. "Please don't feel you must speak of your history with Miss Wells if you do not wish to. I did not mean to pry."

He sighed. "After keeping it to myself for two years, I feel a sudden urge to divest myself of the burden. I hope you don't mind."

"I would hope that you consider me your friend, albeit a newly minted one," she said.

He nodded. "I do." To his surprise, he was indeed beginning to think of the blond Incomparable that way, despite the fact that he had sworn to avoid glittery women such as she when he was in Town. Well, he reminded himself, he'd just sworn not to marry one. There was no reason he couldn't have one as a friend.

"Well, then. As your confidante, I stand ready to hear the whole tale." She smiled as they reached the shore and began to follow a worn, dusty path below some willows.

"It is not a long one, nor a terribly thrilling one. It would make a terrible play, as it would start and end in one short, foolish act."

She nodded but said nothing. When the silence lengthened, he took a deep breath and continued.

"Miss Wells and I met at a house party in Gloucestershire. I was there for the hunting, as was she. But while I was hunting fox, she was hunting peers."

"So she had decided to use her considerable physical attributes to climb the social ladder?" Lady Cassandra had cut right to the heart of the matter, as she was so skilled at doing.

"Exactly so. And, to my misfortune, I found my better judgment clouded."

"You would not be the first gentleman to find

himself in such a position when confronted by a pretty lady." Her smile was self-mocking. "I have found myself in the same situation on the other side of the table, if it is not boastful to say so."

"It is not boastful in the slightest, Lady Cassandra. You are far fairer than Miss Wells, and have twice her strength of character as well," he said with a bit more force than he had intended.

She greeted this declaration with a startled look. "You are very kind. But we have digressed from your story."

"Ah yes. Georgina." He held a low-lying branch aside so that Lady Cassandra could pass by without trouble. The action had the added benefit of shielding his face, so she could not see how discomfited he probably looked after praising her so directly. "We got along well at the house party, or so I thought. I invited her and her mother to visit me several weeks later, and she accepted with alacrity. As it turned out, she had lived for several years not far from Winchfield Hall, although we had never met in our youth. She was delighted to have the chance to visit old friends." He paused. How innocuous that sounded.

"Was the visit a success?"

"It was, at first. As we both enjoy riding, we explored much of the estate. In the evenings, I arranged a few small supper parties and even found enough willing guests for a modest dance." In fact, the neighborhood residents had been astonished and delighted to find him hosting social occasions at Winchfield Hall. Years ago, the old house had often been the scene of joyous parties. Since his parents had passed on and Elinor had eloped, he had had neither the skill nor the desire to organize such amusements. But with his housekeeper's help, he'd managed quite well—or so he'd thought.

"After several weeks, I felt I knew Miss Wells well enough to consider offering for her. She had indicated to me, in both subtle and direct terms, that she would be amenable to such a proposal—although perhaps I misread her interest." So often in the years since the affair, he had reexamined his actions and her words, and every time he had decided that he could not have possibly mistaken her intentions. She had wanted him to offer.

"Generally, a lady is fairly forthright on matters of such import," Lady Cassandra said. "And she must have known what you had in mind when she accepted your invitation to visit."

He skirted a puddle in the path. "I believe she did. In any case, I rode into Dorchester to retrieve my mother's betrothal ring from our man of business, who has most of the Winchfield jewels in a vault for safekeeping."

"And did you indeed offer for her?" Lady Cassandra asked after a moment, her voice rich with sympathy.

"No, thank heaven. That was the only bright spot in the whole debacle." He inhaled a deep breath of fresh air redolent with the heavy scent of lilacs. "Her father is deceased, so I had planned to ask her mother's permission on the evening I returned from Dorchester. However, when I arrived at Winchfield Hall, it appeared that my guests had departed for the afternoon. My groom reported that Mrs. Wells had gone to visit a friend, and I assumed that Miss Wells had accompanied her." Now came the part of the story that always made him feel ill. How could he have been so blind?

"But she hadn't?" Lady Cassandra prompted.

"No. She was still in the house. In the breakfast room, to be precise, entertaining—a visitor."

"One of those old friends she'd hoped to see in Dorsetshire?" From Lady Cassandra's tone, she had a very good idea how the rest of the story would unfold. It was unfortunate that she had not been at Winchfield Hall at the time to warn him. He had not foreseen it at all.

"Yes. A surgeon's son from a nearby village. They had known each other when they were young and had corresponded since. Mrs. Wells, though, had greater ambitions for her daughter, feeling that she could parlay Georgina's looks into a very comfortable future for herself and the children who remained at home. A surgeon's son could not provide the future that Mrs. Wells—and Georgina, to be fair—envisioned." He stopped and leaned again one of the willows that trailed its leaves in the sparkling water. "Miss Wells was not averse, however, to availing herself of the gentleman's other . . . charms."

He felt like a complete prig as he told this part of the tale. But how else was he to describe the scene in the breakfast room that afternoon to a gently bred woman like Lady Cassandra? For all her Town gloss, she was still an unmarried female. He felt the warmth of a deep flush rising up his neck, and he tugged at his haphazardly tied neckcloth.

To his intense relief, she held up a hand. "I believe I can infer—in general terms, if not the specific details—the scene you stumbled onto between Miss Wells and her old friend. May I assume that it was a tableau such as would have forced most gentlemen to do the honorable thing and marry the lady in question?"

"It was." Thank goodness he did not have to spell it out.

"In your own house." Lady Cassandra muttered a very unladylike word of disgust. Ben's surprise at her language must have registered on his face, for she added, "Just because I am not supposed to say such words, my lord, does not mean I am deaf. I have heard them, and in some situations no milder words will suffice."

His bark of laughter broke the tension he had felt at relating this story. "You may be an Incomparable, but you are also an Original."

At this comment, she beamed. "Why, thank you! I would far rather be the latter than the former. But again, we are digressing. Would you like to tell me what happened next?"

Part of him wanted to, and part of him shied away from revealing the humiliating denouement. In the end, he decided that speaking of what had happened might help him erase it from his mind. Certainly keeping to it to himself for two years had done nothing to lessen its hold over him.

"When I discovered the pair, I naturally assumed that Georgina would be embarrassed, but that was far from the case. 'I see you've stumbled on to my little secret,' she said in that bright little voice of hers. 'I would have told you sooner or later.'"

Lady Cassandra caught her breath. "She is certainly self-possessed."

"That is not the half of it." Ben began walking again as he remembered, as if he could leave the wretched scene behind them on the river path. Lady Cassandra fell into step beside him. "She'd planned to tell me after we were betrothed—when it was too late to escape honorably—that she fully intended to maintain her, um, intimate friendship with Stephen Cooper in the future, no matter whom she wed. Cooper, it turned out, was in Dorsetshire for only a brief time, visiting his family. He spends most of the year in London, and she intended to consort with him here."

Lady Cassandra's jaw was hanging open in a most unladylike fashion. "She planned this? Not only planned it, but openly admitted it?"

"Yes. In fact, let me see if I remember her words precisely." His hesitation was for show, as in fact he would never forget her cutting comment. "I believe she said, 'Live year round in the backwaters of Dorsetshire with no one but a bug-loving bore for company? You must be more naïve than I thought.' At that point, I suspect she knew I would never offer for her, so she felt she had nothing to lose by speaking her mind."

His companion laid a hand on his arm. He could feel the warmth of her skin through the layers of damp superfine and linen. "What sort of woman would think such things, let alone give them voice?"

"A woman reared largely in Town, where wit is valued above kindness."

"I understand, now, why you so abhor casual cruelty."

He shrugged. "There is nothing like being mocked in one's own breakfast room in front of a stranger to make one a crusader for uplifting talk."

She shook her head. "I am sorry you had to endure such a scene."

To his own surprise, he chuckled. He had never been able to laugh about that day. "It was embarrassing, to be certain, but if that is the worst I must endure in this life I shall have had a fairly carefree existence.

The least-tried soldier or sailor in the late war likely faced more distressing events than that on his first day in uniform." That was true, he realized, even though he had never put his shame in that sort of context before. Certainly Georgina's words had sliced painfully into his sense of self-worth, but they had been only words. He had let them fester in his brain for far too long.

"That is a most sensible approach," Lady Cassandra said. "I don't know many men who could be so forgiving."

"Believe me, until this moment, the last thing I felt toward Miss Wells was forgiveness. But talking about it has, somehow, lightened my burden. And seeing her today made me realize anew that she did me a favor by speaking so candidly. If she had tried to cover up her indiscretion, to apologize and promise that it would never happen again, I might well have overlooked it and offered for her anyway. And our brief encounter today reminded me just what a mistake that would have been. She is far too much of a sharp-edged Town lady for a shambling country gentleman like me."

"Do not judge yourself so harshly!" Lady Cassandra exclaimed. "You may prefer the country to the city, but you are far the better man. Better person, I suppose," she amended with a smile.

Ben hadn't realized it, but they had stopped walking again and were now standing under a large oak tree. Sunlight filtering through the wind-rustled leaves made shifting patterns on Lady Cassandra's fair hair and pale pink gown. For a brief, wild instant, he thought she looked almost like a fairy princess, before reason took hold and he realized it was just a trick of the light.

She was just another beautiful, polished Town belle—one who was more empathetic and intelligent than most he had met, but still a Londoner through and through, from the ends of her perfectly coiffed curls to the hem of her fashionable gown.

He cleared his throat. "Thank you for saying that. I value your good opinion."

"I'm pleased that you felt comfortable enough in my company to tell me the story. I shall certainly give Miss Wells the cut direct from now on."

"No, please don't do that," he exclaimed. When she tilted her head inquiringly, he added, "Such treatment would only create questions. People would wonder why you were treating her so. It would be impossible to explain without ruining her reputation."

"It seems to me she did quite a good job of that all on her own—well, with Mr. Cooper's help." Her small smile was without humor.

"Perhaps she did, but I have no wish to extend the damage. I just wish for her to leave me in peace, and to avoid her at all costs."

"I shall do as you wish, although I would rather see her punished for using you so ill."

"Retribution solves nothing. Believe me, I know the futility of carrying a grudge. I have lost a decade of my sister's company because I was too proud to bend."

Silence sifted down on them like the sunlight and a few leaves that the breeze had shaken loose from the tree. Beside them, the river burbled over a ridge of smooth stones. Eventually, Lady Cassandra said, "The shadows are growing long. I expect the rest of the party will be eager to return to London before the hour grows too late. And I know there are several, at least, who have some last-minute preparations to make for Lady Farnham's ball."

"I had forgotten that that was tomorrow night. Is it true that it is usually a very grand affair?"

Lady Cassandra laughed. "One of the grandest of the Season. I have known ladies to fuss for a solid year over their costumes. Masquerades are somewhat out of fashion these days, but Lady Farnham's is more popular than ever. Are you planning to attend?"

"Yes, although never having been to a masquerade, I am not at all certain that my costume will be up to snuff. I am wearing—"

"No, no, don't tell me! The fun of trying to guess which of your friends is wearing what is part of the excitement of the evening."

"But won't you see me before we leave? I was assuming we would all ride together."

Lady Cassandra shook her head. "For years, Elinor, Richard, and I have had a custom of departing separately for the ball. It is a bit of harmless fun. It is but a short ride from our house to Lady Farnham's, and John Coachman is used to our little game. He simply makes the trip several times, with one of us on each trip. A footman accompanies us to the door."

"I see. So I may not ask what you shall be garbed as tomorrow night?"

"You may ask, but I shan't tell you." She smiled. "You shall just have to guess along with the rest of the assembled company."

He suspected that he would be able to pick her out of a crowd no matter what her disguise. Even if she covered up that glorious hair with a dull brown wig, and foreswore her usual stylish garments for a witch's rags, he would recognize the way she walked and the way she stood, he was certain. He had always had an uncanny eye for the most beautiful woman in a room.

It was a tendency he would just have to continue to curb. Encountering Georgina this afternoon had been the strongest possible reminder that no elegant city woman would ever be happy in Dorsetshire, particularly with an eccentric scientist.

"You were right a few minutes ago, when you said it was getting late," he said, his voice a bit gruff. "We should be getting back to the others." Before he could change his mind, he turned and led the way back toward the sunny meadow, where he could just barely make out the footmen packing up the remains of the picnic.

CHAPTER EIGHT

Ben took a deep breath as he strolled north along a narrow street whose name he could never remember. The unusual heat had finally broken, and today felt almost as fresh as a spring day in Dorsetshire. It would have been quicker, he supposed, to get from Conduit Street to Oxford Street by following New Bond Street. But he had developed an odd fondness for Hanover Square. Even though the park behind the tall iron railings consisted largely of open grass, and even though it was closed to all but residents of the square, just looking at it made him feel as though he had not left the countryside utterly behind. It was pleasant to see a flat surface in London that was not covered with cobbles and horses.

He approached the little square and observed the park through the fence for a few minutes before continuing on. It was important to reach Oxford Street before the shops closed for the day, as he wanted to find a few last baubles for his costume for the Farnham ball this evening.

Never in his life, Ben thought, had he spent so many of his waking hours focusing on his appearance. He had just come from Weston, the tailor whom Blythe had recommended so highly. Tyson had been delirious when Ben mentioned he was getting a bespoke coat from the famous shop.

"I have read about Weston," the valet had burbled with more enthusiasm than Ben had ever seen him show. "He was a great favorite of Brummel—before Brummel fled to the Continent, of course. I am certain you shall not be disappointed."

And he hadn't been, Ben reflected as he moved away from the park fence and continued his walk along the west side of the square. The coat had fit like a second skin—not surprisingly, since he had endured three fittings. The tailor was sending it ahead to Blythe House. It was too bad, really, that he could not wear it to the masquerade tonight. But it would not fit at all with his costume.

After much deliberation a few days earlier at a costumer's in Covent Garden, he had selected the garb of a Turkish sultan. The rich silk robes and elaborate turban seemed so exotic that he could not resist. It was the sort of thing he would never, in a thousand years, have the opportunity to wear in Dorsetshire.

To his great surprise, he was greatly looking forward to the ball. He wondered what Lady Cassandra planned to wear. Something dramatic and beautiful, he had no doubt, since those were the chief features of her daily wardrobe.

He stopped short and leaned against a lamp standard. Why on earth should he care what Lady Cassandra sported? If he was concerned about any lady's costume, he should be wondering what Miss Lewis planned to wear. To his astonishment, Miss Lewis was intending to come to the party, despite the crush that was expected. "I shall be able to leave before the unmasking at midnight. No one will know me and I can simply drift along the edges of the crowd without speaking," she'd told him at the picnic. "Masquerades are wonderfully liberating."

Perhaps that was what attracted him so to the idea of this party. For once, he could dispense with being the Earl of Winchfield. He had never become quite accustomed to the deference others showed him merely because of his title. Even Weston, who counted some of the most powerful men in England among his customers, had been quietly obsequious, Ben thought as he exited the square and continued north along Harewood Place. At the masquerade, it would be a blessed relief to be just another party guest.

Within moments, he reached Oxford Street. As he turned left into the busy thoroughfare, he almost collided with a man in a tall beaver hat.

"My apologies, sir," Ben began, but then he stopped as he recognized the gentleman. They had met a few months ago in Dorsetshire. "Simpson!"

"Winchfield! What the devil are you doing in London? I didn't think you ever ventured further than Portsmouth." Sir Anthony Simpson extended his hand.

"Even a country eccentric needs to see the lights of the capital once in his lifetime," Ben replied as they shook hands.

His companion laughed. "Well, it is most fortuitous that I ran into you. If I'd known you were in Town, I would have paid you a call earlier."

Ben was flattered but puzzled by the man's interest. They were not well acquainted. "Oh?"

"You're interested in biological studies, are you not?"

"Yes." Ben stepped aside to allow two stately matrons to pass by, followed by several footmen loaded down with packages.

"Well, as you know, I have done a few studies in that area myself. A friend from my club invited me to a meeting of a new scientific society that Charles Goodale is founding."

"Charles Goodale!" Ben knew he probably sounded like a schoolboy, but he couldn't keep the admiration from his voice. Goodale was one of the foremost scientists in England. Ben had read his recent monograph on the migration patterns of songbirds. It was an impressive piece of scholarship.

"So you've heard of him."

"Of course." Ben leaned against the wall of a nearby shop. "I would think a man of his abilities would have no need of a society to support his efforts."

Simpson shrugged his narrow shoulders. "I suppose everyone enjoys the opportunity to discuss their great interests with like-minded people. Anyway, I thought of you the moment I heard about it, but I assumed you were still moldering in Dorsetshire."

Why did everyone in London assume that Dorsetshire was as remote as the moon—even those who had been there? "For the minute, I'm moldering in Mayfair."

"You seem to have honed your wit since coming to Town."

Simpson's comment startled him. Had he really?

"But to return to my point," his friend continued, "would you be interested in accompanying me to the meeting next week? A great many scientists of all abilities are in Town for the Season, so it's an unprecedented chance for us to get together and talk about our studies."

"I would be delighted." *Delighted* seemed too mild a word for the tremor of excitement Ben felt at the thought of discussing his research with his peers, and learning of their investigations in return. This was the sort of opportunity that never came his way in Dorsetshire.

"Excellent. I shall send the particulars to your residence. Where are you staying in London?"

After supplying the information Simpson sought, Ben took his leave. In an elated haze, he strolled down Oxford Street. Perhaps this trip to London would not be completely wasted after all. Even if he did not meet a marriageable lady, he had made another connection of a completely different sort that might prove fruitful.

So absorbed was he in his thoughts that he didn't see Lady Louisa and her brother until it was too late to conceal himself in a shop doorway. He suppressed a groan as the siblings bore down upon him.

"Good afternoon, Lord Winchfield!" Lady Louisa exclaimed. "What a pleasure to see you!"

As they exchanged pleasantries, he resolved to be cordial to the pair. Just because Lady Louisa counted Georgina Wells as a friend did not make her a pariah. Hell, he'd considered *marrying* Georgina, so he was no better judge of character than Lady Louisa was. It was no crime to choose one's friends poorly.

They chatted for several minutes about mutual acquaintances. Then Lady Louisa asked whether Ben had seen the morning newspapers.

"I glanced at them briefly, but I was out and about fairly early this morn," Ben said. "What is there of import?"

"A most interesting story. A select committee has been appointed to look into the matter of chimney sweeps. Did you know that children as young as four have been crawling around in the chimneys of London, all to earn a few pennies?" Lady Louisa's voice was laced with outrage.

Perhaps he had misjudged her after all. Most society ladies would have no more concept of the lives of London climbing boys than they would of the habits of a Calcutta punkahwala. He wondered if Lady Cassandra ever gave even passing thought to the news of the day.

"I had not heard about the new committee, although I did know about the climbing boys. We have them in the countryside, too, although they are much rarer. As I understand it, many boys in London are forced into the life by unscrupulous men who only want to exploit them."

"That is what this morning's article alleged," said Lady Louisa.

As they continued to discuss the committee's work and other current events, Ben's opinion of Lady Louisa improved further. It was true that she could be somewhat shrill and voluble, and that she seemed far too enthusiastic about Georgina Wells. But at least there might be some possibility of building a strong friendship with her, as he feared he might never be able to do with the timid Miss Lewis. He knew better than to expect love from a society marriage, but friendship would be a definite advantage.

Within a few minutes, they parted. Lady Louisa and her brother were likewise engaged in finding a few furbelows for their costumes. With a smile that showed she did not expect an answer to her question, Lady Louisa asked what he would be wearing to the party. He declined to answer, as did she. "La, let us just say that I will appear in a guise you would never expect," she said with an odd little laugh.

They agreed that they would merely try to spot one

another that evening, and use the timeworn greeting "I know you" if they did indeed encounter each other in the throng.

Feeling oddly cheerful about the evening ahead, Ben continued on his way toward a jeweler's shop where, he hoped, the elaborate stickpin he had seen earlier in the week would still be in the window. It would make the perfect finishing touch for his ensemble.

Cassandra was sitting at a desk in the front salon, absorbed in revising the second act of her play, when she heard Lord Winchfield's voice at the front door. To her consternation, her heart gave an odd little skip at the sound. The earl had a most unsettling effect on her. The sooner he was married and back in Dorsetshire, the better.

"Good afternoon," he said as he entered the room. "Have my sister and brother-in-law left you to your own devices?"

She smiled as she laid down her pen. "They have indeed. Actually, they invited me to accompany them on their calls, but I wanted to work on my play, so I remained at home. Usually I write in my room, but the light was so lovely here that I decided to move."

"Is the play coming along well?" he asked as he dropped onto the blue divan opposite her desk.

"Tolerably. Your suggestion yesterday has spurred me in an entirely new direction."

"You mean my comment about the theme?"

She nodded. "I cannot believe I was so obtuse as to not see it before, but the reason the play was not working was that it was far too similar to every other light satire produced in London for the last half century. It is making fun of the same foibles in the same way. But after you suggested that I find a focus for the dialogue, I decided to expand the role of one of the minor characters, Sir Humphrey Mills. He was supposed to be just a foil for the other characters, but the more I wrote about him, the more interesting he became."

"How so?" he asked as he leaned forward to pluck a biscuit from a tray on the low Sheraton table. The housekeeper had brought enough sweets for an army when Cassandra had rung for a simple cup of tea, so there was a great deal left over.

Cassandra could have said that Mills became more and more interesting as she modeled him more and more closely on a new acquaintance—namely, the Earl Winchfield himself. But making such an admission would open up entire other avenues of conversation, down which she had no desire to travel.

The more she tried to deny it, the more she was forced to admit that she was becoming ever more fascinated with Lord Winchfield. Why he held such interest for her, she could not have said under oath. He was as far removed from the type of gentleman who usually caught her eye—witty *bon vivants* like Perry Russell—as the dun earth was from the bright sky.

And yet she had lain awake half the night remembering the quiet confidence with which he had strode into the river to rescue Alice, and the self-deprecating humor with which he had downplayed his role in the drama. Perry, she was certain, would have dined out on the story for months, embellishing it as he went until it would soon have been known about London that he had rescued the entire crew of the *HMS Victory* from the iceberg-dotted waters of the Thames.

There was just something solid about the earl that

she had found in few other London gentlemen. She grimaced as her thoughts began spinning in the same vortex they had the night before. Yes, Lord Winchfield was admirable. And attractive. And available. And to her great surprise, he was not nearly as stodgy as she had once thought. But the one thing that was certain was that he was a countryman at heart. Any woman who married him would be lucky to see London again in her lifetime, unless she came alone, and Cassandra had no interest in the sort of marriage where the partners were husband and wife in name but lived separate lives in reality.

Marriage. She was insane to even be thinking along such lines in terms of the Earl of Winchfield. Not only was he not the sort of gentleman she preferred, she was also not the sort of lady he was seeking. She was neither meek nor malleable.

"Lady Cassandra?" His biscuit half raised to his lips, he was looking at her with concern. She realized to her embarrassment that she had not answered his question about Mr. Mills, the character in her play.

"I have just made him more of a human and less of a stock character," she said. "Once I started trying to determine *why* he acted the way he did, he became far more alive."

"And what *has* made him such a stick?" he asked, with an odd gleam in his eyes as though he knew just on whom she was modeling the character. She could not let him guess.

"A variety of factors," she answered airily. "But I don't want to bore you—"

"It wouldn't bore me in the slightest." He smiled and bit into the gingersnap. "Mmm, these are just like the ones our late cook at Winchfield Hall used to make."

"I believe Elinor asked Cook to look up the old recipe," Cassandra replied. Then, in the hopes of distracting the earl from talk of the character's personality and motivation, she added, "I think the main thing that is helping me shape the play is a comment you made once about ants."

"Ants? You have found a way to work insects into a satire of the London Season?" His expression was so droll that she laughed.

"Not directly. But the other night you were telling Elinor something about queen ants that stuck in my mind—that everyone thinks the queen runs the anthill, but in reality she is just the . . . the spur for the whole society. She lays the eggs but does not direct the action."

"That is true, insofar as ant experts have been able to tell. But how on earth does that relate to your play?"

"I've reconceived Mills as a queen ant. He is not the central character of the play, but his actions have repercussions that affect everyone."

Lord Winchfield smiled. "Did you know that ants appear to communicate without words? Scientists have no idea how they do it. But they must, because they act with a high degree of coordination when they build a new colony or forage for large pieces of food. Perhaps their communication is similar to the silent communication that keeps the wheels of London society moving?"

She grinned. "You mean the speaking glance that passes between mother and daughter when a potential suitor enters the room? Or the way a gentleman's stance alters slightly when a man he considers a scoundrel gives him the cut direct?"

"That is it exactly, Lady Cassandra. You see, we are

not so different, you and I. We are both avid students of society. It is just that the societies I observe are contained and, to a large extent, knowable. The *ton* is small, I'll grant you, but I doubt I shall understand its intricacies were I to stay here ten years."

"What has you so puzzled, Lord Winchfield?" She rose slightly, shifted her chair so that she could see him better, and settled back into it.

"Well, Almack's, for one. Why on earth is the place so popular that vouchers are as valuable as gold? All I was able to observe was a drafty room filled with anxious misses and bored gentlemen, who to a man said they were desperate for a glass of ale and would much rather have been playing a round of faro in White's."

Cassandra's shout of laughter inspired an answering smile from Lord Winchfield. "People do not go to Almack's for fun. It is a duty, rather like attending Sunday services and visiting one's cranky Aunt Harriet. If one hopes to marry, one goes to Almack's, just as one goes to Tattersall's to buy a horse."

"Miss Lewis also compared Almack's to Tattersall's, and I must admit I agree with you both. I half expected several of those mamas to ask me to open my mouth so that they could check my teeth." He plucked another biscuit from the rapidly emptying plate. "I suppose they were wise to do so. If I keep eating biscuits at this rate, I suspect I shall have no teeth left by the time I am forty."

Again, Cassandra laughed. How had she ever thought him stuffy? He just needed a focus for his wit, and it appeared that he was his own favorite target. "I think your teeth are safe for the time being. But to return to our earlier subject, I suppose you are right. We are both scientists, of a sort. But my laboratory is a drawing room while yours is—well, come to think of it, I don't even know where you study ants. Do you just stroll around your fields, scanning the ground for likely looking piles of sand?"

He smiled. "I did at first, but now I build controlled environments in my barn. That way, it is easier to work at night and when the weather is poor. I have a fairly extensive set of lamps out there, and the servants know not to bother me when I'm absorbed in my work. I work at night more often than not, as during the day I am often consumed with estate business."

She had a sudden picture of him out in his barn, his jacket off and his sleeves rolled up as he leaned over some large box, studying his experiment, the candlelight glinting off his hair. Disgusted with herself for romanticizing such a pedestrian, mundane thing as staring at anthills, she changed the subject.

"Here I am badgering you with questions about ants, and I have not even asked you how your walk in Mayfair was. Did you find the accessories you wanted for your costume?"

If he was nonplussed by her change of topic, he gave no indication. "I think so. Truly, I cannot remember when I went to so much trouble to get ready for a social occasion. But I gather it is the done thing. I met Lady Louisa and Lord Halmond in Oxford Street, and they, too, were madly combing the shops in search of baubles."

Cassandra frowned. "For the largest city in the world, London is sometimes entirely too small for my liking. I could last the rest of the Season without setting eyes upon Lady Louisa, and not be sorry."

He leaned back in his chair. "What is it about Lady

Louisa that irks you so? She seems pleasant enough, even if she is a bit unpolished and her choice of friends leaves something to be desired."

"I wish I could say what, specifically, makes me feel she deserves a wide berth. It is just a feeling I have that she is a loose cannon." She bit her lip, unwilling to say more for fear that Lord Winchfield would berate her once more for finding fault with others. "I do not wish to tell tales out of school, my lord, but I would urge you to treat her with caution. There is a rumor about that she is on the hunt for a fortune."

"She would not be the first lady of quality to pursue such an aim during the Season, and I doubt she will be the last."

"That is true, but her family is in particularly desperate straits, which I fear may lead her to take particularly desperate measures. As a wealthy earl in Town for the known purpose of finding a wife, you are a highly visible target. I would strongly urge you to be cautious."

He shook his head. "Thank you for the warning. You are much more knowledgeable in these areas than I. But since I outweigh Lady Louisa by at least four stone and am probably at least a foot taller, I doubt she will be throwing a butterfly net over me and packing me off to Gretna Green any time soon."

Cassandra laughed. He was right—she was probably being unreasonably nervous. Just because she did not like Louisa Dennis was no reason to suspect her of being of unsound character. As if by mutual consent, they let the subject drop and moved on to more congenial topics. But in the back of Cassandra's brain, worry continued to flicker like a dying candle brushed by a breeze. How was it that Lady Louisa always seemed to be exactly in Lord Winchfield's path? It must be simple coincidence, she told herself as she picked up the bell to ring for more tea.

CHAPTER NINE

"Do you know me?"

Cassandra had pondered the question—a standard masquerade greeting—many times this evening, as she had made her way through Lady Farnham's soirée. She had already identified Richard, who was sporting a powdered wig in his guise as Louis the Fourteenth. Elinor was here, too—she had heard her sister-in-law's voice a few times, but hadn't been able to pick her out of the glittering throng. She had seen no sign of Lord Winchfield yet.

Cassandra surveyed the man who had greeted her and quickly decided he was not the earl, as he was of average height and portly build. A rich red velvet tunic stretched from his throat to his knees, capped with a royal blue velvet coat of the same length, trimmed with gold braid and what appeared to be ermine. His legs were encased in white stockings. Around his neck hung a regal-looking gilt chain, and on his head he sported a tam-o'-shanter, also made of velvet and ermine. His face was concealed by a beautifully embroidered silk mask.

"You are Henry the Eighth, I believe," Cassandra said with a grin.

"Very good, my dear, very good. You are one of the

few people in this benighted assembly with any grasp of historical costume," the heavy-set man boomed. "And you, I see, are Diana the huntress."

For her costume, Cassandra had taken the current passion for classical style one step further than usual. She wore a simple white satin sheath from shoulder to toe, tied with a length of gold cord at her waist. She had debated leaving one shoulder bare, as the classical statues portrayed women, but decided that the ancients could do as they wished but she should not tempt the wrath of the goddesses of the *ton*. Across the shoulder that should have been bare she wore a strategically draped garland, which was pinned securely to the waist of her gown. In her hand she carried a small bow, while on her back she bore a quiver of arrows. Agnes had pinned her hair up into a complicated topknot, and despite Cassandra's elaborate feathered mask, most of her acquaintances in the crowd had determined her identity on her hair alone—although Perry, the naughty man, had said her dress left little to the imagination and had thus revealed her to him.

So it was quite possible that the portly king before her knew who she was. She, however, could not place him.

"I am indeed Diana," she confirmed.

"Here to hunt big game among the idle rich?"

A member of the *ton* would be unlikely to make such an observation. Interesting. "Since I *am* one of the idle rich, it would seem that I should not need to don a costume to do that."

"I would not exactly call you idle, Lady Cassandra. For an apparent lady of leisure, you have managed to create a substantial body of captivating plays."

Who on earth was he? It wasn't that Cassandra had kept her writing hobby a secret. She was not ashamed of it. But she hadn't discussed it with that many people outside her family, Perry, Lord Winchfield, and a few others.

"And I am most curious to hear about your new satire, *The Gentleman's Dilemma*," he added.

That was the new title of her work in progress, which she had changed just before sending a letter of inquiry about the project to one of London's most successful theater managers. She had mentioned the revised title—spurred by her new focus on the character of Sir Humphrey Mills—to almost no one else.

"Mr. Fisher?" she asked, hardly daring to breathe. Reginald Fisher was an immensely powerful person in the London theater world. Could he really have read her plays and found them "captivating"?

"The very same," he said, removing his curious cap and bowing deeply. "It is an honor to meet you, my lady."

"The pleasure is all mine," she said, hoping he could see her smile through the feathered mask. "But how did you know who I was?"

"I hazarded a guess at first. I knew from the society notes in the London newspapers that you were tall and fair. A few questions to the appropriate people, including our surprisingly voluble hostess, reassured me that I had indeed guessed correctly."

Cassandra congratulated herself on resisting the temptation to don a wig for the festivities this evening. She had dismissed the idea for fear that such a disguise would be uncomfortably warm.

"I should have known you for a theater person the

moment I saw your costume," she said. "It is quite the most elaborate ensemble in the room."

He chuckled. "People with blunt may hire all sorts of secondhand costumes from the shops in Covent Garden, but we theater folk always keep the best ones for ourselves. There have to be some advantages to being in this business."

Cassandra's heart was exploding against her ribcage like bubbles in a kettle. Reginald Fisher had taken the time to seek her out, and he had said something kind about her plays! Perhaps her dream of becoming a produced playwright wasn't the castle in the air she had often feared.

"Well, you certainly make a convincing Henry," she said, speaking the first thought that came to mind. She had to say something to fill the growing silence while she processed this remarkable turn of events.

He laughed, a great echoing chortle. "This girth once served me well in playing this very role. But I am past my days on the stage now, and prefer to work behind the scenes, discovering London's best new talent and putting their works on the stage."

Cassandra held herself very still.

"I thought this party would be an excellent opportunity to meet you in person, seeing as our worlds seldom intersect," he said. "I could hardly ask you to meet me at Boswell's, now could I? Tick, tack, tock, your reputation would be ruined."

The fabled club for writers and artists was indeed far beyond the pale for women of any sort, but particularly so for women of the *ton*. "That is true."

"And I, for my part, am not much taken with the custom of visiting the quality and nibbling on tiny biscuits and tea," he added. "Not that I am customarily welcomed in most *ton* homes to begin with."

"You would be most welcome in mine! Well, my brother's home, as that is where I reside while in London."

He sketched a tiny bow. "That is very kind, Lady Cassandra. But I thought that this rather theatrical evening would be the best opportunity for us to meet on neutral ground to discuss the ways we might work together. Perhaps, once you have decided whether I am an utter reprobate or not, we may forge a more formal working relationship."

"Of course," Cassandra murmured, her mind racing ahead. A working relationship! That sounded most promising, almost as though he envisioned a long-term association. Perhaps she could truly make writing plays her life's vocation. "But I am certain I shall not find you a reprobate."

"I am disappointed. It is rather a badge of honor among thespians to be considered a scoundrel."

"Well, then, by all means, I deem you a rogue of the first order," she replied, liking the odd gentleman more by the minute. He seemed to share her peculiar sense of humor, which could be why he was the first theater manager in London ever to have shown an interest in her plays.

"Very good. You have learned the first rule of etiquette of the theater world, my dear!" the manager crowed.

"What is that?"

"That the theater manager's whims are to be respected in all matters. Now, about your scripts," he said, leading her over to a pair of gilt chairs at the edge of the crowded ballroom. "We don't have all evening to discuss this, as the bell shall ring at midnight and we shall have to scurry back to our respective worlds. So tick, tack, tock, my dear."

Twenty minutes later, Cassandra and Mr. Fisher had agreed on a price for one of her early scripts, a satire called *The Winthrop Affair,* provided she would make some small revisions.

Cassandra could barely contain her glee. After all these years of scribbling in private, she would actually see one of her plays produced on a London stage! It was all she could do not to bolt from her seat and seek out someone with whom she could share the news.

Mr. Fisher had also offered some excellent suggestions for *A Gentleman's Dilemma*. To her relief, he agreed that the character of Sir Humphrey Mills was an excellent fulcrum on which to rest the play.

"People are tired of seeing the witty characters as the focus. Making the country gentleman the lead is a nice variation—if you can accomplish it while still amusing the audience," he said as he stood to take his leave. "He must be reputed to be a stick, but he cannot be too sticklike, shall we say, in the execution. It will be a delicate writing job, but I think you have the talent to make it work."

"Thank you, Mr. Fisher," she said, rising as well.

"If ever you wish to consult me on any matter of craft, I put myself at your disposal," he said. "Now that we have met, I assume that I will be welcome to call upon you at Blythe House?"

"Most certainly. You would have been welcome in any case."

"Couldn't know that, couldn't know that," he said in the repetitive cadence she'd quickly learned was an unconscious tic. "Some of these Mayfair ladies are too high in the instep to receive a mere baker's son in their homes, even if they aren't too mighty to pepper me with dreadful scripts written on scented paper. I do not mean you, of course," he hastened to add. "Your offerings were neither dreary nor perfumed."

She laughed. "No offense taken."

As he bowed, he added, "I am serious, Lady Cassandra. I believe in working closely with 'my' playwrights to shape their works. I am glad to hear that you customarily remain in London for the whole Season, and frequently beyond that. While it is possible to do revisions by post—indeed, I do them frequently—it is much simpler to be able to speak in person when revising a play."

She nodded. The opportunity to have someone as renowned as Mr. Fisher as her mentor was one she could not possibly pass up. Thank goodness she had a permanent invitation to make her London home with Elinor and Richard as long as she wished. And thank goodness she had no responsibilities that would take her outside the city during the Season.

Once Mr. Fisher had taken his leave, she set off in search of Elinor, who would be delighted by this news. Unfortunately, the crowd had grown even more substantial in the minutes she had been chatting with the theater manager, and Cassandra had not yet determined what costume Elinor was wearing. From her sister-in-law's broad hints, Cassandra suspected that she was dressed as some sort of servant, but the ballroom was swarming with masked women in the garb of dairymaids and housekeepers.

She had just spotted a woman about Elinor's height, dressed as a parlormaid, when she collided with a tall gentleman in flowing silk robes. An enormous turban jingling with paste jewels made him appear even taller.

"Please forgive me," she said, drawing back. "How clumsy of me."

"The fault was mine," came the response in a low, rich baritone that she instantly recognized. "Your costume is lovely, Lady Cassandra."

"And yours is exceptional, Lord Winchfield," she said, delighted to have stumbled upon him. "If you had not spoken, I should not have known you at all."

If his voice had not given him away, the grin visible beneath his gilded mask certainly would have. Again, she felt the odd little stammer of her heart that that smile always provoked.

"Thank you," he replied. "I am a neophyte at these affairs, so I am glad that my ensemble is up to scratch."

She wondered whether she should share her momentous news with him. Instantly, she dismissed the idea. Despising the theater as he did, he probably wouldn't think the news was very important. Worse, he might try to dissuade her from working with Mr. Fisher, feeling it was beneath her. She was so excited that she couldn't bear the thought of him throwing cold water on her moment of success.

"Are you enjoying the party?" she asked, anxious to distract herself from distressing thoughts of a potential argument.

"Very much," he said. "I have danced with the most unusual assortment of belles, from Cleopatra to Marie Antoinette." He moved back a pace or two and observed her disguise. "But I must say that your costume is one of the most beautiful I have observed this evening, and you do it justice."

The simple compliment disarmed her much more

than Perry's effusive praise had done earlier in the evening. "Thank you. And may I return the sentiment? With your height and frame, you are well served by your costume. Most gentlemen here could not carry off the guise of a Turkish sultan convincingly."

He shrugged and turned up his palms. "I feel rather like an overly upholstered divan, but it is great entertainment to stroll about in anonymity. For once, I have not been besieged by pushy mamas and their breathless daughters. Speaking of which, have you determined which of these ladies is Miss Lewis?"

"I believe she is the shepherdess standing near the fireplace." Cassandra indicated a slim woman in a beige dress with a light blue cloak and a staff, who was chatting with uncharacteristic animation to a man dressed as a pirate and sporting a fearsome black mask.

"I should go over and make myself known to her." Resignation, not interest, tinged Lord Winchfield's voice.

"Why, if you do not wish to?" she asked impulsively. "You can always claim that you were not able to identify her in the crowd, if she later asks why you did not approach her."

"That is true." He sighed. "But as enjoyable as it is to flit about the edges of the assembly, I suppose I should continue to focus on my primary purpose here in London."

She hated to see him so unenthusiastic. "Take a holiday from your cares, just for this evening," she urged. "That is, after all, the whole point of a masquerade: to act the part of someone you are not, just for the night."

He hesitated for such a long moment she feared she

had offended him. But then, to her surprise, he
laughed. "Perhaps I have become too focused on this
whole affair of marriage. It would be good to set it
aside for a short spell. You are wise, Lady Cassandra.
And with that resolve, I now have several dances to
arrange at my whim, instead of in the service of duty.
Would you care to be my partner for the next one?"

"I would be delighted. But are you certain you dare?
The last time we danced together, I was not at all congenial." She still felt embarrassed about the scene she
had created on the dance floor at Elinor's rout.

"Nor was I, but I have put that out of my memory
and so should you." He smiled. "But to ease your
mind, I happen to know that the next dance is to be a
country dance, so there is no danger that we shall col-
lide with the other guests while attempting to waltz in
these costumes."

"That does ease my mind," she replied, even as a
glimmer of regret seized her. It would have been enjoyable to waltz with the earl again. He was not the
most accomplished of dancers, she had to concede,
but it would have been enjoyable to spin about the
floor in his arms once more, now that they were on
friendlier terms.

She was being disingenuous. It would have been
more than *enjoyable* to waltz with the earl, she had
to admit.

"It seems that the dancers are assembling. Shall we
join them?" he asked, extending his elbow to lead her
onto the dance floor. She placed her hand on his
sleeve, permitting herself a frisson of pleasure as she
sensed the warmth of his skin below the rich fabric of
his costume.

It was such a shame, really, that he could not learn

to endure London. If he were more interested in living in the capital, then maybe—

She cut that thought off before it could fully flower. There was no sense in pursuing such foolish fantasies. The Earl of Winchfield was determined to leave Town as soon as possible. And she was determined to stay—more strongly than ever, after her conversation with Mr. Fisher.

She repressed a sigh. Even if she and the earl shared a fondness for London, so many other things made him a completely ridiculous object of her affection. First, if his comments at the picnic had been any indication, he viewed lady playwrights as only slightly better than Covent Garden lightskirts. And second, he was a man who clearly relished getting his way in all things. As she relished the same thing, it seemed unlikely they could ever have a completely amicable relationship.

As they moved into position, she turned her thoughts to more congenial matters, such as her exciting conversation with Mr. Fisher. Unfortunately, her delight in the theater manager's offer was dampened, just slightly, by the realization that she was reluctant to share her joyous news with the earl. It would have been so much fun to do so.

Ben congratulated himself on remembering all the complicated steps to the dance as he and Lady Cassandra wove their way among the other couples. As he raised his hand above his head and she took it, he glanced at her eyes, so startlingly blue behind her feathered mask. In those eyes, if he was not mistaken, he saw a hint of the same affection he was beginning to feel for her.

It was ludicrous for him to be drawn to Lady Cassandra, he thought as he turned her lightly and propelled her in the direction of a gentleman dressed as a Roman centurion. If he had sought the length and breadth of London, he could not have found a lady less suited to his purposes. A belle of the *ton* with suitors galore—he had spotted at least three men this evening vying for her favors—would be certain, eventually, to find more compelling company than he. And while it had disturbed him somewhat when he realized that Georgina Wells had such a fickle heart, he knew it would devastate him if Lady Cassandra strayed. He already valued her far too much to countenance that.

"Sir?" He returned his attention to the dance and saw that the lady to whom he had turned was waiting for him to take her hand and rotate her toward the opposite line of dancers. Still distracted, he did so.

"Do you know me, sir?" she asked.

He had not given her more than a passing glance until this moment, but now he observed her more closely. She was wearing an elaborate Renaissance costume of some sort that included a long, heavy-looking cape. He wondered why she had not discarded it, as the temperature in the ballroom had soared to uncomfortable levels.

Her costume gave him no clue as to her identity, but then he spotted a stray wisp of red hair that had escaped from what was obviously a dark wig. "Lady Louisa?"

"My disguise is revealed," she said with a small laugh as she returned to her partner. Assessing the build and stance of the centurion, Ben guessed that he was Lady Louisa's brother, Halmond.

In moments, Ben was face-to-face once more with

Lady Cassandra. "Lady Louisa seems to have an un-canny ability to find you in a crowd," she murmured.

"Please, Lady Cassandra—"

She laughed. "Do not fret, my lord. I have no in-tention of starting an argument out here on the dance floor. I was merely making an observation, and I should have been wise enough not to go even that far." She watched as Lady Louisa and Halmond, who had moved one couple up the chain of dancers, exe-cuted a pretty turn.

He followed her gaze. "She is behaving with per-fect decorum tonight."

"Of course. I did not mean to suggest otherwise."

A few moments later, the music finished and the perspiring dancers began to disperse. Ben was about to ask Lady Cassandra if she would like a glass of ratafia when Lady Louisa materialized at his side.

"It is very hot in here," she said in an oddly strangled voice. No wonder she felt constricted, he thought, con-sidering the long cloak still wrapped securely around her neck. "Would you care to accompany me to the garden for a breath of fresh air?"

He supposed he should. Despite his earlier words to Lady Cassandra, he felt he should be using this party to further his wife-hunting efforts. Perhaps the degree of playfulness afforded by their costumes would give him the chance to get to know Lady Louisa a little better, and to determine whether her motives were as suspect as Lady Cassandra feared. He looked at his sister's relative, only to see that Lord Halmond had already engaged her in conversation. Nevertheless, he could not simply abandon her on the dance floor. "Lady Cassandra, would you like to ac-company Lady Louisa and me outside for some air?"

Beside him, Lady Louisa stiffened. She must have been offended by his efforts to include Lady Cassandra in their walk. Perhaps she had hoped to have his exclusive company, but she was the one who had rudely approached him before he had had a chance to return Lady Cassandra to the side of the dance floor, as etiquette required. So she should not be surprised, nor offended, to find he had extended the invitation to his partner.

"Lady Cassandra has just agreed to accompany me to the gallery. I hear that the Farnhams have a most intriguing artwork collection," said Lord Halmond.

Lady Cassandra shot Ben a look that, even through her mask, indicated quite clearly that she would far rather be in the garden than in the gallery. "Lord Halmond is right. So thank you for your invitation, my lord, but I shall have to decline."

The two couples strolled through the ballroom to the corridor and made their way down the stairs to the ground floor. After easing their way through clots of people to reach the back of the house, they parted company in the somewhat less crowded gallery. Halmond and Lady Cassandra stopped to admire a portrait near the terrace, while Ben and Lady Louisa continued through the French windows and down the stairs into the dim garden. He could smell, rather than see, some early blooming roses.

After the close heat of the packed house, the chill air of the garden was a slight shock. The sky had looked to be threatening rain when Ben had arrived at the house, and the drop in temperature and the strong breeze presaged a storm at any minute. Glancing around, he noticed that most of the other party guests had apparently come to the same conclusion.

The garden—large by London standards—was almost deserted.

"Perhaps we should postpone our walk?" he said, glancing up at the sky and noting that no stars shone.

"Nonsense, Lord Winchfield! I am perishing of the heat, and it will be delightful to have the garden to ourselves," Lady Louisa said, her voice even shriller than normal. "If the rain begins to fall, we will not have far to dash to reach the house."

He still felt dubious about the wisdom of staying outdoors, but he acquiesced. She seemed so intent on remaining outside that it seemed rude to argue.

They followed a small brick path to a stone bench, onto which Lady Louisa dropped none too gracefully. "Lud, it is a relief to sit down. The shoes I selected to complement this costume are terribly uncomfortable." She stretched her feet out in front of her and toed off first one shoe, then the other.

"I'm sorry to hear that," he said, settling onto the other end of the bench as he tried to ignore her unladylike behavior with her shoes. He leaned back slightly, only to feel the prickle of a thorn against his scalp. Twisting around, he noticed that a large, overgrown rose arbor concealed the bench from the rest of the garden, making their seating area uncomfortably private. "Lady Louisa, this situation feels most improper."

"Don't be foolish, Lord Winchfield. I trust you to be honorable. Please just humor me. My feet are in excruciating pain, and I really need to rest for a moment or two longer."

"Of course." He could not like it, but neither could he suggest that they return to the house until she felt refreshed.

She reached up and removed her mask, and took a

deep breath. "That feels better. This mask is so hot. Is yours not unbearable?"

"It is a bit uncomfortable, now that you mention it." He pulled it from his face and dropped in his lap. She was right. It was good to be rid of the heavy contraption.

She did not reply to his statement, nor did she offer another observation. Eager to keep the conversation going, Ben finally asked whether she was enjoying the masquerade.

"Tolerably well," she said, fiddling with the strings that appeared to secure the cloak around her throat. "Lady Farnham's annual party is always diverting. Are you finding it so?"

"Most assuredly." They lapsed into silence, something he had never before experienced in Lady Louisa's presence. "Your costume is very elegant."

"Thank you."

"It is a shame that it is hidden by that long cloak."

"If I can get this annoying bow undone, I shall resolve that problem. Would you be so kind as to assist me, Lord Winchfield? The strings appear to be knotted."

"Uh, certainly." Awkwardly, he reached across the bench and began to examine the bow. It looked uncomplicated. As he looked up to tell her so, he saw a thin sheen of perspiration on her cheeks. "Are you all right, Lady Louisa? You look a bit flushed."

"I am fine," she reassured him. "Have you ever seen such a lovely moon?"

"A moon?" He let the bow drop and shifted his gaze to the sky, puzzled. Just two minutes earlier, not even a star had been visible.

At his side, he heard a swish of fabric. Out of the

corner of his eye, he saw Lady Louisa's cloak slip from her shoulders. It was good that she had figured out how to untie it, as he felt devilishly uncomfortable fiddling with the knot himself.

"Frederick!" she screeched, her cry so loud that he reared backward. "Help, help, Frederick!"

Help? Why the devil was she shouting for help? And why was she calling her brother's name? Shifting his attention back to his companion, Ben took in the scene in an instant, and felt his stomach plummet to his boots.

The dress Lady Louisa wore beneath her cloak was gaping open, a jagged tear running from the shoulder to the deep neckline. His first instinct was to look away, but horror kept his gaze locked on hers.

She flashed him a small, triumphant smile, then resumed her cry of distress. "Frederick, help me! Help!"

In desperation, he swung his arm around her shoulders and clamped a hand across her mouth. She struggled against him, but he held firm.

"I may be just newly arrived from Dorsetshire," he hissed in her ear as bile rose in his throat, "but even I know what you are trying to do. And believe me, it will not work." He suppressed a very strong urge to shake her.

Lady Cassandra had been more perceptive than he. She had tried to warn him that something like this would happen, but he had brushed away her concerns. He had thought he had everything within his control. When would he ever learn that nothing in life is fully predictable?

Beneath his hand, Lady Louisa squirmed. Ben debated whether it would be more prudent to release his hand so that he could flee as far from her as possible, or to lean in closer and tell her exactly what he thought of her scheme to entrap him into marriage. Deciding on the former course, he looked wildly about the walled garden, as if a magic door through which he could escape would suddenly appear. *Think, man, think!*

When he heard something crunch in the arbor behind him, all the air rushed out of his lungs and he struggled to breathe. He realized his arm was still about Lady Louisa's neck.

"What a very interesting position to find you in, Lord Winchfield," drawled Viscount Halmond as he emerged from behind the tangled rosebushes, his mask dangling from his fingers.

CHAPTER TEN

Cassandra had been admiring a pretty portrait of Lady Farnham's daughters and sipping a glass of punch when Lord Halmond excused himself. She had been glad to be rid of him, truth to tell, as he was a mediocre conversationalist—as taciturn as his sister was talkative. It was pleasant to have a moment of solitude to simply look at the paintings and think.

Once again, she turned over in her mind the extraordinary conversation with Mr. Fisher earlier in the evening. He had said that it might be possible to mount a production of *The Winthrop Affair* before the Season was out. "Buy the play, rehearse the play, perform the play," he'd said. "Tick, tack, tock. No time to fuss. Just costs money I don't have. We can use the sets from a play I'm producing now. Drawing room farce. Very similar."

His offhanded manner had astonished Cassandra. He had given her her life's dream on a silver salver, and he had acted as though he had done nothing more remarkable than ask her to dance.

The portrait gallery had started to empty as the musicians in the other room began tuning up for another dance. There were perhaps only a dozen people left in the room, most of them clustered around the fireplace

on the wall furthest from the French windows. The
heavy silk draperies billowed into the room as a cold
gust of wind rattled the glass.

No wonder everyone was gathered at the opposite
end of the chamber, Cassandra thought. That breeze
was chilling. Lady Farnham would probably appreciate it if someone closed the windows.

As she moved toward the exit to do just that, Cassandra heard an odd sound from the garden, almost
inaudible over the whistle of the wind in the eaves of
the old Farnham mansion. She paused and listened.
There it was again. It sounded like someone shouting
for help.

Hadn't Lord Winchfield and Lady Louisa been des-
tined for the garden when they left the dance floor a
few minutes ago? With dread twisting her stomach into
a tight knot, Cassandra hefted up her trailing hem and
bolted in a most unladylike manner for the French windows, sailing over the threshold like a steeplechaser.

Outside, she immediately saw the source of the
noise. At the far end of the garden, Lord Halmond
was dashing toward a large arbor. Her foreboding
growing, Cassandra followed him.

He spoke to someone on the other side of the arbor
in tones that did not sound promising. She could not
hear most of it, but she did catch the last word,
"Winchfield."

Sprinting across the final stretch of grass, she felt a
light drop of rain on her shoulder, followed by another.
A strong blast of wind scattered dry leaves across her
path and tugged at the mask covering her eyes. It would
not be long before a downpour began. With luck, she
would have time before the rain came to fix the disaster she imagined transpiring behind the arbor.

Out of breath, she slowed her pace so as not to alert Lord Halmond of her presence. Tiptoeing behind him, she rounded the arbor on the opposite side and peered around the thicket of roses, but her mask made it difficult to see in the gloom. She removed it and dropped it on the ground.

She stifled a groan as she took in the scene: Lady Louisa's torn dress, Lord Halmond's theatrical glower, and Lord Winchfield's genuine anger. The earl's fists were clenched at his sides, and his face was tight. Anyone who did not know him would assume that he had ripped Lady Louisa's dress in a fit of pique. But Cassandra did not entertain that thought for one second. Such an action was so far from what she knew of the earl's temperament that it was ludicrous to even consider it.

Lord Halmond, however, seemed more than prepared to come to that conclusion. "Ah, Lady Cassandra," he said. "How fortunate that you've arrived. Now I have another witness to this appalling situation."

Cassandra raised her eyebrows. "Indeed. It *is* appalling that a lady would stoop to such measures in order to trap a husband."

Now it was Lord Halmond whose skin looked stretched too tautly across his high cheekbones. "If you were a man, I would call you out for that remark."

"Fortunately, I am a lady, and so have no fears about speaking the truth." She turned to the earl, whose slight smile of thanks confirmed—even though she had needed no confirmation—that Lady Louisa had tricked him. At that moment, several heavy drops of rain plopped onto her neck and scalp, followed by an ominous rumble of thunder far in the distance. "Lord Winchfield, I see no need for us to continue this conversation with these fortune hunters. I believe you have promised me a dance?" She inclined her head toward the house.

"But what about my sister's honor?" bellowed Lord Halmond.

"Lady Louisa should have given more thought to that before coming to a masquerade dressed as a harlot." Cassandra's voice was cool.

"Someone garbed as immodestly as you are, Lady Cassandra, should not cast stones. Have you decided that it's time to show the *ton* a little more of your—attributes—in a final attempt to avoid being left on the shelf?" The viscount's mouth was curled into an ugly sneer.

People could become so foolishly vindictive when their wishes were thwarted, Cassandra thought.

"Don't say another word, Halmond, or *I* will call you out." The earl spoke for the first time since Cassandra had happened upon the scene, and his voice was as hard as steel.

"What does it matter to you, Winchfield? Like Lady Cassandra, I only speak the truth." His mouth twisted into a menacing smirk. "Unless you have designs on the fair Incomparable yourself? If that's the case, you're more foolish than I thought. The great Lady Cassandra has turned up her nose at half the Corinthians in the *ton*. She certainly isn't going to settle for a dull countryman like you."

"Your sister seems more than happy to settle for a dull countryman," Lord Winchfield pointed out.

"Louisa doesn't have the options Lady Cassandra has. Lack of fortune makes a lady much less choosy, believe me."

"It's too bad her brother gambled away her dowry

and left her in such an inconvenient position." Cassandra knew her remark would only fan the flames, but she could not help herself.

"I was cheated!" Lord Halmond shouted. "Demmed scoundrels at Boodles. I should have known better than to play anywhere but White's. They took away my birthright!"

The wind had died down, as it often did just before the rain began in earnest, and the garden was as silent as if it were holding its breath. Cassandra held hers. Lord Halmond's voice would be clearly audible from the portrait gallery. If anyone of a curious nature were still in that chamber, it would be only moments before the little group in the garden had company. If Cassandra was to contain this situation, she would have to do so quickly.

"My lord," she began, praying that her gift for quick thinking would not fail her now, "perhaps you were cheated, but that is not relevant to the point at hand. There are many gentlemen with substantial fortunes in London this year. Surely your situation is not so dire that you cannot wait until at least the end of the Season—"

"You know nothing of our situation!" Lady Louisa cried. "If I am not married within the week—"

"Louisa, be quiet!" the viscount roared.

"Is there a problem, Lord Halmond?" came a woman's voice from the steps leading up to the portrait gallery. Cassandra's heart plummeted to her toes as she recognized the loud tones of their hostess. Lady Farnham was one of the most notorious gossips in London—and, curiously, a stickler for proprieties as well.

"Lady Louisa, please, for heaven's sake, put your

cloak back on." Cassandra knew she was begging, but she didn't care. Once Lady Farnham saw the sordid little tableau behind the arbor, there would be no chance of saving Lord Winchfield from either a terrible scandal or a disastrous betrothal. "If you have one shred of decency—"

"It's fine for you to talk of decency—you who have sneered at me at every opportunity!" Lady Louisa cried. "I know you think you are better than I, but you're not! You're simply a high-in-the-instep lady whom fortune has blessed with a fairer face and plumper purse than I. You do not understand the first thing about what it is like to be me." Tears were running down the red-haired woman's face, mixing with the rain that was falling more steadily now.

"We should go inside," Cassandra said in a rush. "Pull your cloak on to protect yourself from the rain, Lady Louisa. Once we are indoors, I shall apologize for any wrongs I have—"

"What on earth are all of you doing out here in the rain?" Lady Farnham asked as she swept around the corner of the arbor. Her question drowned out the rest of Cassandra's desperate plea. "I heard you when I came in to the gallery to check that the maid had closed the French windows." As she glanced at the four people gathered in the arbor, her face registered first confusion, then shock. Her gaze swiveled to the earl, who returned it steadily.

Good for him. He has done nothing of which he needs to be ashamed.

"Lord Winchfield." The older woman's voice sounded like that of a minister in the midst of a full fire-and-brimstone oration. "Would you care to explain to me why Lady Louisa's dress is in such a shocking state?"

"Lady Louisa and her brother are trying—" Cassandra began, but Lady Farnham held up a hand. Lord Winchfield glanced at Cassandra and gave his head a minute but unmistakable shake.

"Thank you, Lady Cassandra, but I addressed my question to Lord Winchfield." Their hostess rested her hands on her ample hips and fixed the earl with a stare that permitted no evasion. "What have you to say?"

Lady Cassandra held her breath. What the earl had to say could very well determine the direction of the rest of his life.

Ben swallowed as he stared at the fiery avenging angel standing before him in the rapidly worsening storm. Lady Farnham had every right to look thunderous; the situation before her must seem self-explanatory. Although, as he had learned from studying the natural world, the most obvious explanation for a situation was rarely the correct one.

He glanced at Lady Louisa. As the rain began to soak her costume, she looked even more pathetic than she had when this debacle had begun. Streams of water dribbled from her tangled coiffure, and the shreds of her bodice were plastered to her skin. Her lower lip was trembling in a most unpropitious manner.

What financial straits could possibly be so awful that Lady Louisa and her brother would have concocted such a pitiful scheme? Whatever trouble they were in, it was very serious.

"Lady Farnham," he began, "the situation is not as it appears. Believe me, I know how scandalous it must look."

"Adducing scandal here does not require a huge

leap of deductive reasoning. Seeing how it could be anything else, however, would take a depth of imagination I'm afraid I don't possess."

"Well, Lady Farnham, it is actually quite simple." Before he explained the situation, however, he hesitated. Peering again at Lady Louisa, he saw an emotion on her face that hadn't been evident before. Fear. Not just fear, but pure terror, as she glanced at her scowling brother. What hold did the viscount have over her? And what would happen to her if this plan did not succeed? She sent him a pleading glance.

There was nothing for it. He could not leave her to her fate, which he suspected would be a very unpleasant one. In any case, honor decreed that he must offer for her. It was not the sort of marriage he'd hoped to contract, but it appeared to be the match that had been forced upon him. At least he would not have to return to Dorsetshire a bachelor. That was something, he supposed.

"Lord Winchfield? What is this simple explanation you mention? It had better be persuasive, or else Lady Louisa—and you—may well find yourselves social pariahs before this evening is over."

He felt the rest of his life yawning before him like a featureless, endless chasm. He took a deep breath and stepped from certainty into the void. "It is a common story, Lady Farnham. Lady Louisa and I came out to the garden for a bit of privacy. I took a few more liberties than I should have. The lady protested."

To his right, he heard a sharp, indrawn breath. He knew it was Lady Cassandra, and he knew that if he glanced at her, he would lose heart for the course he had set out on. But there could be no turning back now.

"Go on." His hostess's voice was unyielding.

"I was ungentlemanly in my reaction to her resistance. It was wrong, and I wish to take full responsibility for my actions. If her brother will allow me, I would like to ask for her hand in marriage."

From the corner of his eye, he saw Lady Louisa slump against her brother, likely with relief.

"No, Ben, you can't!" Lady Cassandra cried.

His given name on Lady Cassandra's lips almost undid him. Suddenly, with a clarity that almost made him gasp, he saw all at once how his life could have been different.

He had been an utter fool.

It had been madness to pursue colorless women simply because a beautiful one had scorned him. He should have known better than to apply the lessons of one isolated incident to a whole group. That was one of the basic errors that all the scientific texts warned scholars to avoid.

Lady Cassandra might be beautiful like Georgina Wells—in fact, she was ten times more so—but she had as much in common with that scheming hoyden as a sleek greyhound had with a boxer. Both were the same species, but utterly unlike in temperament and breeding.

He had thought he wanted a plain woman. But what he had truly desired was a *smart* woman. And Lady Cassandra had shown her intelligence in many ways since the day they had met—not least in her efforts to extract him from this disaster tonight.

Even though she was committed to her life in London, he could have at least tried to engage her affections. He thought of the future they might have shared, if he could have convinced her to spend most of the year in Dorsetshire. That was a huge leap of faith, but he permitted himself the luxury of imagining her as the mistress of Winchfield Hall. She would have filled the largely neglected, silent rooms with color and laughter and people—all the things that had been missing from his life since Elinor had eloped. It would have been wonderful. It was too late now.

"Yes, I can," he said, as he turned to look into Lady Cassandra's shocked face. Her expression called forth a deep pang of wistfulness that he tamped down. "I cannot leave Lady Louisa alone to face the wrath of the *ton*."

"But you did nothing wrong!"

"You think the state of Lady Louisa's dress is *nothing*, Lady Cassandra?" Lady Farnham's tone insinuated that anyone who thought something so ridiculous was almost as far beyond the pale as Ben was. He could not let this monumental disaster swallow Lady Cassandra as well.

"She did not mean to imply that," he interjected, hoping his voice did not reveal his rising panic. "She is not apprised of all the elements of the situation."

"Enough of this chattering," Halmond put in. "I give you *carte blanche* to offer for Louisa."

Ben turned to the woman who had trapped him into a situation that was becoming more distasteful by the second, but which honor required him to bring to only one possible conclusion. "Lady Louisa, would you do me the honor of consenting to marry me?"

"I would be delighted, thank you, my lord," she said, fluttering her eyelashes at him in a dreadful parody of flirtation, reminding him of the day he had met her at the circulating library. "And if I may be so bold,

I would like to suggest that we be married by special license, to forestall any unnecessary gossip that may attend our betrothal."

"Gossip? Why should there be gossip? We are the only witnesses to your current state, and none of us shall talk, I am sure."

"Oh, I shall take this story to the grave!" Lady Farnham declared. Behind her, Ben saw Cassandra rolling her eyes. So their hostess was not known for her discretion, it appeared.

Damn. Not only was he going to have to wed this tricky harridan, but he was not even going to be permitted to have time to get used to the idea. Even if Lady Farnham wasn't the gossip Lady Cassandra's expression had implied, Ben wouldn't put it past Halmond to threaten to spread his own stories of the scandal. He had an uneasy feeling that the viscount would put his greedy hopes for this match ahead of even his sister's reputation and comfort.

This trip to London had not turned out precisely as he had planned. He had found love, he thought as he glanced at Lady Cassandra. The only trouble was, he had found it just half an hour too late.

CHAPTER ELEVEN

"Don't be preposterous, Ben. You simply *cannot* marry Lady Louisa, after she has used you so ill." Elinor's tone brooked no argument. "You are an earl, after all—not some country squire she can push about for her own ends."

"I can and I shall," Ben said. "I have offered for her, in front of three witnesses. There is no going back."

"If asked, I shall say you were delusional," Cassandra remarked from her chair by the window in the drawing room at Blythe House. It was almost three in the morning, and her patience was ebbing as the night wore on. She agreed with Elinor that Lady Louisa should not be rewarded for her trickery, but on one point Lord Winchfield was completely correct: He had offered for the bluestocking, and there was no way he could honorably withdraw that offer.

It was a dreadful dilemma, to be certain. But something about the situation prickled at the back of Cassandra's mind, like an itch she could not scratch. Something was not quite right.

"No one shall ask you," Lord Winchfield retorted. His words were clipped, but his expression when he looked at her was soft. It was a strange look, one he had given her several times since the disaster in the

Farnham garden. She could not quite interpret it, but if pressed, she would say he looked almost regretful.

"Are you quite prepared to go through the embarrassment of having the banns read? I assume the ceremony—if one may call it that—will take place at St. George's?" Elinor's voice was cold. St. George's, on the edge of Hanover Square, was the parish church for most of the wealthy denizens of Mayfair. It was *de rigueur* for the most stylish weddings to take place there.

"There will be no banns. The chit wishes to be married by special license, to avoid further scandal. Can't see why she cares *now* about scandal," he muttered. " 'Twas she who created the furor in the first place, by wearing that ridiculous costume and luring me into the garden."

As he continued to rail against the perfidies of Lady Louisa, Cassandra's mind fastened on to one thing the earl had said. "Can't see why she cares *now*." That was the crux of what had been bothering her since Lord Winchfield's startling proposal, Cassandra realized: the sudden escalation in Lady Louisa's desperation.

Her brother had wagered the deed to their unentailed town house in a marathon gambling session at Boodles last year. The pair had been living with relatives until they had moved into rented quarters in Chelsea several weeks ago, but as far as Cassandra had heard, no further major blow to their fortunes had befallen them. It was well known around Town that Lord Halmond had a small income of several thousand pounds a year, which he was using largely to pay off his substantial gambling debts. By all accounts, he had managed to stay out of the gaming hells since losing his house. So nothing had changed substantially in the last year.

So why, suddenly, was Lady Louisa desperate enough to risk her pride and her reputation to trap Lord Winchfield into marriage? And why was she so avid to be married with such haste? The story of the scene in the garden would circulate regardless, whether the marriage took place in three days' time or a month's time. One would think that Lady Louisa would prefer to drag out the preparations for the wedding to reap the full society benefits of a betrothal to an earl. There would be celebratory parties in her honor, a flurry of dress fittings, mentions in the newspaper society columns. . . .

Cassandra's whirring mind stopped at that thought. Newspaper articles. Yes, the columnists would definitely sit up and take notice of the wedding of a rich but reclusive earl to a plain girl of no fortune. And even if there were some murmurings in the press about the unusual nature of their betrothal, the bulk of the columns would likely be devoted to substantial discussion of the bride: her coiffure, her dress, her general personality and demeanor. Louisa Dennis adored attention of any sort. Why would she forgo the opportunity to be the toast of the Town to avoid scandalous talk that was likely to circulate—courtesy of Lady Farnham—anyway? It was most uncharacteristic.

"How, exactly, does one go about procuring a special license?" the earl was asking Richard in aggrieved tones.

"It is necessary to apply directly to the Archbishop of Canterbury. His chambers are in Doctors Commons. I shall accompany you there myself tomorrow, if you wish."

"Some company on this devilish errand would be most welcome. Thank you, Richard."

Cassandra noted the earl's grateful smile. The bad blood that had existed between her brother and Elinor's seemed to have evaporated completely after yesterday's picnic. At least one good thing had come out of Lord Winchfield's trip to London.

She watched Lord Winchfield as he paced before the fireplace, running his hand through his dark, curly hair. She had never before seen the composed earl so agitated. If she could find a way to help, she would, even though she doubted he would accept her assistance. Ever since she had witnessed the debacle in the garden, he had been waving off all her suggestions.

She reached for a cup of lukewarm tea that sat on the low table beside her. There was little hope it would revive her or help train her mind on the problem at hand, but at least the action gave her something to do. Rarely in her life had she felt so helpless. It seemed clear that the earl was going to marry that fortune-hunting schemer, and thus doom himself to a life of misery. For a moment, she wished he were just a shade less honorable. But if that were the case, he wouldn't be Ben.

She flushed slightly as she remembered using the earl's Christian name in the garden at Farnham House. The assembled company had looked at her in shock, as well they might. Having heard Elinor call her brother by his given name so often, Cassandra had become used to the sound of it. And in private, when she had entertained fantasies of ways she and the earl could come to an understanding despite their vast differences, she had somehow started to think of him by that name. She had never expected to say it out loud, however, particularly in a public setting.

As he continued to pace, she reflected that the name suited him. Blunt, and sturdy. Reliable. Like the man himself. Just as only Perry could carry off a foppish moniker like Peregrine, only someone straightforward and true could suit a name like Ben.

Do we grow into our names or simply color them by our actions, she wondered, then shook her head. The hour was growing very late, and she was becoming fanciful. Such ruminations would do nothing to help Lord Winchfield escape from his trap. It would be better if she retired to bed and tried to sleep so that she would be refreshed in the morning and better able to consider all the facets of the earl's problem.

She was certain that there was a missing part of this situation that she simply could not see for fatigue. Like the subplot of a play that smoothly brings the main debate into sharper relief, there was some bit of information she did not know that would explain Lady Louisa's actions tonight, which were desperate and bizarre even by the red-haired woman's standards.

Covering her mouth with her hand as she yawned, Cassandra stood. "I am deeply sorry for your plight, Lord Winchfield," she said as she moved past him. She repressed an odd urge to reach out and give his arm an encouraging pat. As she imagined how such an unadvisable action would feel, the hairs on the back of her neck prickled. It had always been clear that Lord Winchfield was a man who spent a great deal of time outdoors engaged in physical activity, and on the few occasions they had danced, she had sensed a strength in his arms that Town gentlemen such as Perry Russell and Edward Symes simply did not possess.

"I confess to my chagrin that I can barely concentrate on the discussion," she continued in a rush, blotting out all thoughts of Lord Winchfield's arms or any other part of his anatomy. "If I retire now, I may have better luck focusing on your dilemma in the morning."

"There is nothing to focus on, Lady Cassandra," he said in a tired voice, looking at her once again with that odd expression. "The deed is done and my fate is sealed. All that remains is to obtain the special license and speak to the rector of St. George's. By this time next week, I shall be a married man."

It sounded so final, she thought as she took her leave and climbed the stairs toward her room. It *would* be final, unless she found a way to stop this idiotic plan that was taking shape.

She had at least as long as it took to procure a special license to figure out just why Lady Louisa was so desperate. It wasn't much time, but it would have to do.

"And why do you require a special license, Lord Winchfield?"

Ben filled his lungs with the stale, dusty air that seemed to pervade every room in Doctors Commons. The room in which he sat looked as though it had not seen daylight since the Reformation—and perhaps it hadn't. Dark red velvet curtains swathed all the windows, and the walls were paneled in what appeared to be rosewood. In the gloom, a few dim lamps burned. The coals in the grate threw out almost as much light. He felt as though he were in a tomb.

To Ben's surprise, he and Blythe were not meeting with the Archbishop of Canterbury himself. Instead, they were closeted with one of his functionaries, Reverend Barrett, who apparently also had the authority to grant special licenses. Reverend Barrett, however, seemed loath to exercise that authority in Ben's case.

Ben spoke carefully, hoping that his answer would appease the archbishop's assistant. "As I mentioned, my fiancée is eager to marry as quickly as possible."

"Would there be a specific *reason* for this haste? A future event for which you want to prepare?" The man's meaning could not be clearer if he had taken out an advertisement in the *Times*. Ben bristled at the implication.

"No." His voice was curt, partly because the very thought of Lady Louisa as the mother of his children made him feel somewhat ill. "My fiancée is not *enceinte*," he added, just to erase all doubt from the unctuous cleric's mind.

"Well, that is a relief."

To us both. "I also need to return as soon as possible to my estate in Dorsetshire, as there are some matters there that require my attention."

"Perhaps you should have concluded your business in Dorsetshire before coming to London."

Ben bit his tongue. He could not fault the man for being condescending, as Ben himself was committing the worse crime of lying through his teeth. He wondered if lying to a clergyman was a more serious sin than telling falsehoods to less holy souls. "Perhaps, but the fact remains that I must leave London quickly, and I would be most appreciative if I could bring my new bride with me," Ben said. He envisioned the long journey back to Dorsetshire in the company of the loquacious Lady Louisa and dug his fingernails into the richly upholstered arms of his chair. Not for the first time, he heartily wished he had not attended the masquerade the previous evening.

Regrets were for weak men, he told himself, repeating an adage his father had favored. Ben had made his decision, and he would uphold it. There was no honorable way to do otherwise. And perhaps, if he was lucky, Lady Louisa would be grateful to him for rescuing her from whatever morass she was embroiled in with her brother. The next time he saw her, he would ask just what it was that made her look at the viscount with such trepidation.

"I'm not sure your situation is sufficiently extreme to warrant the issuance of a special license," Reverend Barrett said, leaning back in his wing chair and folding his hands over an ample belly. "As you attend St. George's, could you not simply procure a standard license from the rector there?"

"I have not been in Town for the requisite four weeks. Nor has Lady Louisa been in residence for a month in her parish in Chelsea."

"I see. So this is a very hasty marriage indeed." Reverend Barrett raised his bushy gray eyebrows, which reminded Ben strongly of dusty caterpillars. "All the more reason for me to consider the matter of a special license with caution." He turned his attention to Richard. "And you, sir? I seem to recall that your wedding was rather unconventional as well."

Blythe flushed a dull red but, to his credit, did not avoid the clergyman's stare. "Somewhat, I suppose. We eloped to Gretna Green. But I must assure you that we have comported ourselves with the utmost dignity since. My youthful actions should in no way influence your decision regarding Lord Winchfield's request."

"As you say. But it appears that your family has a history of rushing into matrimony."

"Lord Winchfield is a family member by marriage only. And I don't see how my actions a decade ago reflect on him now."

The minister drummed his fingers on his belly. "All part of a pattern. That is what we look for when considering these requests. Patterns." He sighed, a gusty theatrical sound that suggested that the weight of the entire Church of England rested on his fleshy shoulders. "I am sorry to say, my lord, that I must deny your request."

Ben blinked. He was not sure whether to be delighted or devastated. Certainly Lady Louisa would not be pleased by this turn of events, and he was certain that she would let him know of her displeasure at some length. But perhaps this delay was a blessing in disguise. It would mean that there was no alternative but to wait until one of them had been in residence a month in London before applying to a local parish for an ordinary license. Lady Louisa had been in Chelsea for three weeks. That would give him a week's grace to determine the reasons for her unseemly haste to wed.

And perhaps, a tiny, dishonorable part of him hoped, to find some way to escape this demmed tangle.

"Well, of course, I was shocked to see such a thing taking place in my garden!" Lady Farnham said as she replaced a small silver bell on a mahogany side table in her drawing room. "I am so glad you came by, Lady Cassandra, as I have been *avid* to discuss the affair with someone, and yet I have kept my promise not to breathe a word of it to a soul." She paused, a frown creasing her round face. "Well, I *did* tell dear Andromeda. And Minerva. But they are likewise sworn to silence."

Andromeda and Minerva could only be the Hulse sisters, Cassandra thought in despair. Their father had been a self-professed intellectual, and had demonstrated his knowledge of science and the ancient world when naming his children. The Hulse sisters were second only to Lady Farnham herself in their fondness for the latest *on-dit*. Lord Winchfield would be very lucky indeed if he had not replaced Lord Byron in the pantheon of *ton* scoundrels before the day was out.

"Lady Farnham, I am here to inform you that Lady Louisa has treated Lord Winchfield most cruelly. As we tried to tell you last night, the situation was not at all as it appeared."

"The way it appeared certainly did not cast the earl in a positive light." Her hostess's lips were pressed together in distaste. "To see poor Lady Louisa in such a state of dishabille, and half drowned in the rain to boot! It was unconscionable. If you had not seen it yourself I would be loath to even discuss it with you, as you are an unmarried lady."

Cassandra put aside her frustration with married people who conspired to keep her innocent of some of the more interesting-sounding facets of life, and focused on the matter at hand. "Lady Louisa put herself in that position, so she has no one but herself to blame."

"Put herself in that position?" Lady Farnham looked toward the door as a maid came in with a tea tray. After directing the servant to place the tray on a low table before the fire, she returned her attention to Cassandra. "Do you mean to suggest that Lady Louisa was wrong to go out into the garden with Lord Winchfield in the first place? Surely, a lady should be able to trust a gentleman to control his . . . urges . . . for the space of five minutes? I hope that society has not come to such a pass that we cannot even rely on the basic civilities."

"Lady Farnham," Cassandra cut in, "Lord Winchfield behaved like a perfect gentleman last night. I would be willing to swear to it on the Holy Bible, if asked."

"How can you be so certain? Did you see them?" her hostess asked as she poured tea from a Wedgwood pot into two matching cups.

"No. But I know Lord Winchfield." She did, in fact, know him very well, Cassandra had realized the previous evening. Seldom had she been so certain that she could vouch for the actions of another human being. Everything she knew about Ben—from his rescue of Alice in Richmond to his efforts to stem Cassandra's habitual criticism of the *ton*'s denizens—reinforced her perception of him as a man of integrity. Even his bull-headed insistence on rescuing Lady Louisa from her own folly fit a predictable pattern.

"I know Lord Winchfield," Cassandra repeated as she accepted her teacup from Lady Farnham, "and I can assure you that he would *never* so abuse a lady's trust and reputation."

"How, then, did Lady Louisa come to be in such a condition?"

"She came to the party that way."

Lady Farnham paused midsip and gasped. "Tore her own dress and plotted to trap Lord Winchfield?"

Cassandra nodded. She had suspected something of the sort, and the earl had confirmed her theory last night.

"My dear, I cannot believe it. What lady would take such a risk?"

"A lady in dire straits. I suspect that Lady Louisa and her brother are in serious financial difficulties."

"Well, of course they are. Did you not know that Lord Halmond lost their house last year in a night of deep play at Boodles?" Lady Farnham shook her head as if disbelieving that Cassandra could be so far removed from the *ton*'s most salacious gossip.

"Yes, of course, but something new must have happened recently. Something they were not expecting, which has made them desperate to engineer a profitable match for one sibling or the other." Cassandra paused a moment to let her words sink in, then leaned forward, setting her teacup on the table with a clatter. "Can you think of anything you have seen or heard in relation to Lady Louisa or Lord Halmond that might have given them cause to panic?"

Asking Lady Farnham to recall gossip was rather like going to the Bank of England and asking a clerk to find some currency. Her stores of half-truths and rumors were prodigious. Cassandra thanked heaven that Lady Louisa had chosen the Farnham masquerade as the setting for her stunt, and that their hostess had been the one to stumble upon the scene. That made it simple to press her for information without the need to describe the affair in the garden to anyone who hadn't witnessed it.

Lady Farnham leaned back in her chair, her teacup

tilted at a precarious angle. It was apparent she had
forgotten all about it in her eagerness to supply some
likely tidbits. "Something about Lady Louisa and her
brother? Let me see. They have not been long in
Town this Season. I know that Lady Louisa was pursuing a Mr. Evans with great fervor during a house
party last month in Oxfordshire. My friend Lady
Trimble was there, and she told me that Lady Louisa
made a complete cake of herself. This Mr. Evans
didn't return her interest in the slightest."

"Mr. Evans? What do you know of him?"

"Very little, I'm afraid. Lady Trimble said he
owned a mine. Or was it a mill? Some sort of business concern." She laughed as she reached for the
plate of sweets and directed a questioning look at
Cassandra. When Cassandra shook her head, her
hostess chose a small biscuit for herself and returned
the plate to the table. "Whatever it is he does, he must
be good at it. He is frightfully rich, apparently."

That was a clue, Cassandra thought. It confirmed
her suspicion that Lady Louisa was desperate for
money. It was Ben's purse, and not his title, that had
attracted Louisa's interest.

"Do you recall hearing that she has made similar
efforts here in Town to engineer a good match? Have
you heard any talk of her spending inordinate
amounts of time with a particular gentleman at a social function, or seeking introductions to powerful
individuals?"

Lady Farnham considered the question as she nibbled on her biscuit. "No, not that I can recall," she
said finally. "But there has been at least one gentleman most determined to find *her*."

Cassandra tilted her head. This didn't sound like

much of a lead, but it might be all she would be able to obtain from this conversation. "Yes?"

"He was at the masquerade last night. I'd forgotten all about him in the ensuing furor." She leaned over the plate of cakes again and deliberated among them. Cassandra stifled an urge to press her to say more.

When Lady Farnham had finally selected a seed cake and a gingersnap, she resumed her former posture and took a deep breath. "Anyway, this gentleman at the party asked me whether I knew if Lady Louisa was in attendance. I said I thought so, but with the masks and costumes it was difficult to be certain."

"Do you know who he was?"

The older woman shook her head. "I'm afraid I don't. My husband invited a number of acquaintances whom I didn't know, and I assumed he was one of them. He was short, I remember that. Barely as tall as I am. He was wearing a domino costume, which made it impossible to identify him. I do recall, however, that his hair was ash blond. His hood slipped back at one point."

A short blond man looking for Lady Louisa. It was the tiniest thread to pursue. "Did he reveal why he was seeking her?"

"Said he was an old friend and that he had not seen her in years. He mentioned that he had recently returned from India, which made sense, as his skin was very brown. It was quite the contrast to his fair hair."

India. That could be useful. Cassandra had heard that nabobs frequented particular clubs. Perhaps Richard could help her track down this new arrival. The fact that he had just returned to England piqued Cassandra's interest. Perhaps his arrival was the spark that had lit Lady Louisa's matrimonial fire. How or why, Cassandra could not begin to guess. Maybe he brought news of a further tumble in the viscount's fortunes, although it seemed they had already plummeted as far as they could go.

"He had a lisp," Lady Farnham added.

A short, ash-blond gentleman with a lisp should not be too difficult to pick out of a crowd in some nabobs' club—if, indeed, he frequented such establishments. This was the most solid hope of discovering Lady Louisa's secret that Cassandra had come across so far.

"Thank you, Lady Farnham. That is most helpful."

"I'm glad to have been of service, my dear. If Lady Louisa has indeed acted as you say—and I do not doubt your word—then it would be reprehensible for Lord Winchfield to be tricked into marrying her. Although I suppose it's too late to think about that now," she added in a pensive voice. "We all heard him offer, and I suspect that Lord Halmond would sue him in court for breach of promise if the earl cried off now. The die appears to be well and truly cast."

"That's true," Cassandra said, rising to take her leave. "But as we've learned already, appearances can be deceiving."

CHAPTER TWELVE

"Bartholomew Dempster," Richard said as he entered the drawing room at Blythe House and dropped on to the chaise longue.

"What a preposterous name. Who is that?" his wife inquired.

Richard nodded toward his sister. "The mysterious blond nabob Cassandra wanted me to find."

Cassandra, who had been staring absently out the window, returned her focus to the room. "Lady Louisa's friend?"

"The same." Richard crossed one booted foot over the opposite knee. "I wasn't able to get into the Expedition Club, of course, as I am not a member, but I asked George Kirkwood for information. I was with George at Oxford, and I knew he had spent time in India and so might be a member of the Expedition. To my delight, I was able to run him to ground this afternoon at Gentleman Jackson's, and he said without a doubt that the man we are seeking is Bartholomew Dempster. He fits all the specifications. He is short and very blond, and speaks with a lisp. He returned from Calcutta not two weeks ago."

"Two weeks?" Cassandra's heart sank. Lady Louisa's efforts to secure a match with Mr. Evans in

Oxfordshire had taken place last month—long before this Mr. Dempster had returned to England.

"Yes. Wasn't that what you asked—to find a man who had recently returned to England?"

She nodded. "But that might be too recent." Taking a moment to consider the situation, she decided that Mr. Dempster was likely not the solution to their puzzle, but he was the only possible clue at the moment. "However, I should like to speak with him anyway. Were you able to determine where he lives?"

"Better than that." Richard grinned. "I found out that he is a very enthusiastic theater patron, and that he intends to go to a performance of *The Academy of Love* this evening."

"How on earth did you discover that?" Cassandra said admiringly. Really, her brother could be most useful, when he put his mind to the purpose.

"George overheard him telling someone at the Expedition that he was avid to see the play, and that he was delighted to be able to see it from a box, as a friend had an extra seat."

Perfect. It should not be difficult to spot a short, blond man in a theater box. The only difficulty would be creating a pretext for a meeting, but there had to be some way to do it. Even a chance encounter in the lobby should be sufficient excuse.

"Thank you, Richard. I doubt this will lead to anything, but Mr. Dempster is the only promising clue I have been able to uncover so far."

"I really think you should change your mind about not telling Ben of your efforts," Elinor said in a worried voice. "He has had a reprieve of sorts, now that the archbishop has declined to issue a special license. The wedding will have to wait a week at least. I suspect he will be interested in any faint chance that it can be called off all together."

Cassandra shook her head. "I do not want to raise his hopes until I have something solid to relay to him." That was part of the reason she was reluctant to inform Ben that she was working to uncover the reasons for Lady Louisa's behavior. The main reason, however, was that she suspected that the earl would not appreciate her attempt to meddle in his affairs and would ask her to stop. Then, of course, she would have to defy him, as she had no intention of stopping. And that would be unpleasant.

There just had to be more to Lady Louisa's desperation than met the eye. And even though she suspected that Lord Winchfield could not be swayed in his determination to marry the red-haired schemer, even when confronted with a rationale for her perfidy, Cassandra had to try. She could not simply stand by and watch him plunge into a miserable match.

"So I am off to see *The Academy of Love* this evening," she announced. "It's an enjoyable play, but I doubt I'll watch much of it. Would you care to accompany me, Elinor?"

"But what of Winchfield? Won't he want to come?" Richard asked.

"Won't I want to come where?" the earl asked from the doorway.

Cassandra hadn't heard him approach. She was surprised, as she had become used to his light tread on the stairs. But when he crossed the room, she realized why she had not heard him. He walked as though in a drugged dream. She had not seen him all day, and she was shocked at the dark circles under his eyes. His night had obviously been as sleepless as hers.

"Are you well, Lord Winchfield?" she asked.

He turned to her with a tired smile. "As well as can be expected, I suppose. I have just been to see Lady Louisa."

"I assume that she was not pleased by the archbishop's decision?" Richard asked.

"That is putting it mildly," the earl said, collapsing into a wing chair with no pretense of grace. He extended his long legs in front of him. "She berated me at great length, and then suggested that if we had to wait a week to get an ordinary license from her parish in Chelsea, we would be just as well to elope."

"Elope!" Elinor cried. "Surely she knows your opinions on that."

"If she did not before, she does now." He rubbed a hand over his eyes. "I informed her that I was willing to save her reputation by marrying her, but I was not about to put the reputation of the earldom in jeopardy by haring off to Gretna Green." He smiled weakly at Elinor. "No offense meant, Ellie. It is just that, as the earl—"

"I know, Ben," she said, crossing the room and kneeling in front of him to take his hand. Cassandra wished she had the right, and the courage, to do the same. "Do not fret. You were right to say no. If it is scandal she wishes to avoid, an elopement would be the last way to do so."

"That is what I thought. Something about this entire affair is deuced odd. If she wanted to avoid scandal, why would she trap me in front of half the *ton* at the Farnham ball in the first place?"

"I've been pondering the same thing," Cassandra said.

Elinor shot her a speaking look, obviously hoping that Cassandra would tell the earl about the mysterious Mr. Dempster. Cassandra hesitated. It seemed cruel to encourage his hopes on such a miniscule pretext.

But then she looked once again at Lord Winchfield's shadowed face. This debacle was costing him more than he was letting on. For a man who prided himself on his honor and integrity, being in the vortex of a *ton* scandal must be particularly hellish.

He would be unhappier still if he discovered that Cassandra was working behind his back to resolve his dilemma. If she had learned nothing else about the earl in the days since he had arrived in London, she had learned he liked to be in possession of all the relevant facts about a given situation, so that he could exert some semblance of control.

She took a deep breath. "There is a very slight chance that I might be able to shed some light on that riddle," she added, and Elinor exhaled a relieved breath.

He looked at her with such hope that she almost wished she hadn't spoken. What if Mr. Dempster turned out to be nothing more to Lady Louisa than an old friend? "I spoke with Lady Farnham this morning, to see if she had heard anything unusual about Lady Louisa or Lord Halmond. She could think of nothing, aside from the fact that a gentleman at the party last evening was most eager to find Lady Louisa." She described her conversation with Lady Farnham, and Richard's subsequent search, which seemed to have uncovered the blond man's identity.

"I propose to go to the theater this evening and attempt to speak to Mr. Dempster, if I can find him," she said. "Perhaps he knows why Lady Louisa has become so rash in recent days."

Lord Winchfield nodded. "Perhaps." His voice was flat. He clearly thought her plan was unlikely to shed much light on the issue at hand, and she could not blame him. She was strongly of that opinion herself.

"Would you accompany me to the theater, Lord Winchfield? There could be more entertainment on the bill than the play itself."

"Certainly, Lady Cassandra. Even though theater has never appealed to me in the slightest, it would be my pleasure to join you tonight. And thank you for your efforts on my behalf. I do appreciate them." Despite the flatness in his voice, she noted once again the odd expression on his face that, since the masquerade, had often wreathed his features when he looked at her. If she had not known better, she would have taken it for respect.

"Miss Lewis!" Lady Cassandra cried as they made their way through the crowded lobby. "How surprising to see you here. I thought you disliked the theater."

The pale young woman looked more animated than Ben had ever seen her. "I am growing to enjoy it," she said with a covert glance at the man at her side. He had the same build as the pirate she had been conversing with at the masquerade. "Mr. Carswell enjoys it greatly."

"Indeed I do," boomed that gentleman.

Once Miss Lewis had introduced them to her companion in a surprisingly steady voice, they parted and made their way to their seats.

"My protégée appears to have found a congenial

match all on her own," said Lady Cassandra as they climbed the stairs to their box.

"She said they had met only a few days ago. Is it not a bit hasty to consider them practically betrothed already?" As soon as the words were out of his mouth, he wished he could swallow them. He was a fine one to talk about strangely hasty betrothals.

If Lady Cassandra noticed his embarrassment, she diplomatically refrained from commenting on it as he held the curtain to their box aside for her.

"It is good to see that this play is still drawing large crowds," she said as they settled into their seats high above the stage. The lofty box was the perfect vantage point from which to survey the assembled audience.

Ben leaned back in his chair and ran a finger around the edge of his neckcloth. Tyson had tied the demmed thing too tight. If and when Ben finally managed to escape London, he would make sure it was a month at least before he had to wrap one of the cursed articles around his throat again.

He supposed Lady Louisa would not approve of that break with sartorial decorum. He suspected there were many things about his life in Dorsetshire that would not meet with his future bride's approbation. With a frown, he dismissed such thoughts. She was the one who had trapped him into this foolish match, and if she rued the consequences it would be her own fault. He would continue to live his life as he saw fit. And if she found herself bored in Dorsetshire, well, she would have to learn to amuse herself.

But perhaps his intended would be happy there in the long run. Perhaps they could make this marriage a proper union, despite its inauspicious beginnings.

He glanced to his side at Lady Cassandra, who was

peering at the boxes on the other side of the theater.
Concentrating intently, she appeared uncharacteristi-
cally unaware of his own scrutiny. Usually so
observant, she seemed instantly to know when his
gaze was upon her. For that reason, he avoided looking at her, as he feared his emotions would show
nakedly on his face.

Tonight she wore a gown of some sort of frothy pink
material, which cascaded about her like a sunset-tinged
cloud. The dress had tiny sleeves and a deep neckline,
revealing a swath of creamy, flawless skin. Despite his
better intentions, he found himself admiring its cut,
which set off her lush curves to advantage. Not for the
first time, Ben reflected that it was no surprise that
Lady Cassandra had earned the sobriquet "Incomparable." She was, without a doubt, the most stunning
woman in this assembly.

Why was it, he wondered, that a plodding countryman like him was inevitably drawn to belles like Lady
Cassandra? Would it not make more sense, from a
natural history standpoint, for dull sorts to be drawn
to less-showy companions, like the plain Lady
Louisa? Ants, after all, did not mate with butterflies.

He sighed. There was no sense trying to fathom the
yearnings of the heart. Much as it pained him as a
man of science to admit it, some things simply could
not be explained.

It was not just Lady Cassandra's pretty face and
form that attracted him, he thought as she scanned the
boxes and then focused her gaze on one of the doors
to the gallery below. Georgina Wells had had both,
and yet he had been unable to look at her again once
she had revealed her true colors. Her beauty had

faded for him irrevocably the day he had come upon her and Stephen Cooper in the breakfast room.

But Lady Cassandra's beauty had only grown in his eyes in the weeks he had known her in London. She was both beautiful and smart, which was unusual in his admittedly narrow experience.

Lady Louisa, on the other hand, did not strike him as a quick study, for all her knowledge of current events. Her ruse last evening had seemed more desperate than clever. There were too many things she had done wrong: her panicked demands for a special license or Gretna Green, her insistence that she was trying to avoid scandal while openly courting it at a crowded masquerade. That alone had alerted him—and Lady Cassandra—that something in her plan was awry.

Lady Cassandra had not only divined that Lady Louisa was acting irrationally; she had also come up with a plan for getting to the root of that odd behavior, and had carried it out without fear for her own reputation. By coming to the fore as his champion, she could well have alienated Lady Farnham.

His companion was still absorbed in assessing the audience, so he continued to observe her. It was a harmless pleasure, he reassured himself, even as he suspected that it was unseemly for a gentleman betrothed to one lady to so enjoy gazing at another.

Lady Cassandra's hair tonight was caught up in a complicated coil. Long gleaming curls, just visible from his vantage point, framed her face. He wondered how long her hair was. He imagined it streaming down over her slim shoulders, where it would be easy to run his fingers through it.

"I think I see him!" she cried as she twisted back in her seat to face Ben. He felt a warm flush creeping up behind his ears and hoped she had not perceived him staring at her like a green schoolboy. As much to conceal his embarrassment as to see the gentleman she had spotted, he swiveled his gaze away from hers and looked in the direction she had last been facing.

"Where?"

"There, in the third box from the left. He is just taking his seat."

Ben looked in the box indicated and saw a slight man placing a tall beaver hat on the floor in front of him. He did indeed have an unusual shock of hair—so blond as to be almost white, which looked odd on such a young gentleman. He straightened before sitting down, and Ben could see that he was not tall. His head barely grazed the shoulder of the other gentleman with him. All in all, he matched Lady Farnham's description well.

Ben glanced again at the other gentleman in the box and smiled. "I believe I may be able to arrange a meeting with our quarry," he said.

"How?"

"The tall gentleman accompanying our blond friend is Sir Anthony Simpson. I met him last year at a horse fair in Dorchester, and I encountered him the other day in Oxford Street."

"What excellent luck! For once, I am very glad that the *ton* is such a limited world."

"As am I. The only difficult thing now will be ensuring that we encounter them in this crush."

"That should not be a problem. I know this theater very well. Just before the interval, we should leave our seats and make our way to the stairway leading down from their box. Then it should be a simple matter for you to call out a greeting to your acquaintance."

Ben nodded his agreement. Now that they had spotted Dempster, it was almost impossible to focus on any other topic of conversation.

"What do you think his relationship is to Lady Louisa?" Cassandra speculated.

"It could be almost anything. He could be a former suitor, or perhaps he wants to collect a debt from Halmond. They might be cousins, for all we know."

"It is curious that he was reduced to asking about her at the masquerade. That makes me wonder whether he has attempted to call upon her in Chelsea and been rebuffed."

Again, Ben admired her quick mind. "I suspected the same thing. It is a most curious situation."

Their speculations ran in similar circles for the next fifteen minutes, until the play began. As the curtain rose, Ben found himself momentarily distracted. He had never had the slightest interest in theater, believing that it was nothing but a group of adults capering about on a stage like children engaging in a game of pretending, but the frisson of anticipation that crackled through the crowd as the play began was almost impossible to resist.

He tried to follow the action and had to admit that it seemed diverting. The lights and the costumes and the laughter of the audience together created an intriguing spectacle. Perhaps another night, he would return and see whether he might actually enjoy the performance. But tonight he could not have told a judge the basics of this play's plot if he had been under oath in a courtroom. His mind kept wandering back to Bartholomew Dempster, even though he knew he was being foolishly hopeful about the secrets the blond man might reveal.

Even if this was the man who was hunting for Lady Louisa, there could be a very simple explanation for Lady Louisa's reluctance to see him, Ben told himself. He might be an old neighbor who had treated her boorishly at a country assembly, for example.

But he kept coming back to the argument Lady Cassandra had laid out in the Blythe House drawing room earlier in the day. Lady Louisa's behavior had become more desperate in the last several weeks. Mr. Dempster had arrived in London in the last several weeks and was eager to find her. There had to be a connection.

Finally, Lady Cassandra nudged him. "I suspect that the action of the play is coming to a head in anticipation of the interval. We should try to make our way across the lobby before a huge crowd prevents us from doing so."

He nodded and rose awkwardly from his chair, sparking several muttered complaints from the patrons sitting behind them.

"Excuse us, please. Excuse us. My companion is not feeling well," he murmured as they shuffled past several other seats and finally reached the curtained door to the box.

"Why should it be I who is feeling unwell?" Lady Cassandra demanded with a grin when they were on the dark stairs leading down from their box, far from the earshot of the other patrons. "Just because I am a lady does not mean I have a faint constitution."

He smiled in return. Her little joke broke the tension that had wrapped itself around his temples since they had first spotted the man who appeared to be Dempster. "Believe me, Lady Cassandra, the last thing I would accuse you of is weakness. You have the strongest character of any woman I have ever met, and I suspect you have the constitution to match." Why the devil had he said that? It was true, but he had had no intention of speaking his mind so bluntly.

She turned to face him, her blue eyes wide. "Why thank you, Lord Winchfield. That was a kind thing to say."

Suddenly, her use of his title irked him unduly, even though it was perfectly proper. "Why don't you call me Ben?" he said on impulse. For someone who had spent a lifetime avoiding rashness, he had an unsettling tendency to speak before thinking when he was in Lady Cassandra's company.

Her eyes widened even further. "I don't know if it would be proper for me to take that liberty."

Something in her expression let him know that she wanted very much to take just such a liberty. He hoped it wasn't simple, misplaced male vanity, but underneath her surprise he thought he sensed a yearning to match his own. Perhaps it was the way she held herself very, very still. He was certain she felt the same strange connection to him that he felt to her.

"You took the liberty last night," he said, his voice low. "When you came upon Lady Louisa and me in the garden."

"I was shocked."

"At my behavior?"

"No." She shook her head. "I knew in an instant that Lady Louisa had trapped you."

"How could you be so certain? You barely know me." Somehow, he sensed that a great deal was riding on her answer.

She looked directly into his eyes. "Sometimes, I feel I know you better than I know myself. We may not be long acquainted, but I know without doubt that you are a decent, honorable man." She paused, then took a deep breath and added, "Ben."

As she spoke his name, their surroundings seemed to fade into nothingness. He could no longer hear the faint voices of the actors on the stage, no longer sense the warm air of the crowded building, no longer smell the peculiar scent that Lady Cassandra had explained was the odor of gaslights. It was as though they were completely alone in the world.

"I appreciate your confidence in me." His voice sounded raspy and strained to his own ears.

"I know it is not misplaced."

Her quiet belief in him unhinged him more than anything had ever done. He had become used to thinking of himself as beneath the notice of many people in society—nothing more than an eccentric countryman who spent his days peering at creatures through a magnifying glass and ignoring the larger world. Georgina Wells had said as much, when she had laughed off his regard as though it were as valueless as a cheap trinket.

To have the respect of someone like Lady Cassandra was a prize indeed. Why had he not realized it until it was too late? Within a week, or two at most, he could well be leg-shackled to Lady Louisa. He could cry off, he supposed, but that would embroil him in a raging scandal.

More to the point, he was not sure he could expose Lady Louisa to the ridicule that would ensue. She had tricked him, and he could not like her for it, but he sensed that the trickery had not been her idea. He recalled the looks she had exchanged with her brother in the Farnham House garden. The ruse to entrap him had not been her idea, he was certain. Her brother had put her up to it, and she feared his wrath if she did not carry through with the plan.

Lady Louisa had enough problems to grapple with, without him leaving her as the laughingstock of the *ton*. He could not cry off. He could not go back on his word.

But looking down into Lady Cassandra's eyes, he very much wished he could do just that. And he wished, devoutly, that he could kiss the Incomparable Cassandra. Just once. Just so he would truly know what he had missed. That would be foolish beyond belief. But, for once in his life, could he do the *wrong* thing?

"Ben?" Lady Cassandra's eyes were concerned. "Are you all right?"

No, he thought. *I am not all right. I am very, very wrong. But this may be the last chance I have in life to throw caution to the wind. Once I am married, I will have to be the soul of propriety for the rest of my days.*

"I'm not sure," he said slowly. "And I'm not at all certain I am the upstanding gentleman you believe me to be." And then, before he could reason his way out of his decision, he placed his hands on Lady Cassandra's bare arms, pulled her gently toward him and kissed her.

CHAPTER THIRTEEN

Propriety was highly overrated, Cassandra thought as she stretched up on her toes to meet Ben's kiss. Waves of sensation, like molten honey, swept through her limbs and threatened to topple her to the threadbare carpet. As much to keep herself upright as to give in to the temptation she had been fighting for days, she laced her hands around Ben's neck. That gave her an irresistible opportunity to bury her fingers in the curly hair at his nape, which she seized without the slightest hesitation.

Something in the deep recesses of her mind whispered that what they were doing was wrong. Wrong to kiss another woman's betrothed. Wrong to kiss a man in a public place. Wrong to kiss a man with whom she could not possibly have a future. If this was wrong, though, why did she feel so utterly secure?

She shivered as Ben deepened the kiss. A self-professed hermit he might be, but he put to shame the few *ton* beaus who had stolen a kiss from her in Seasons past. Never before—no matter how elegant the gentleman nor how witty his repartee—had she felt such an all-consuming desire to fall into a man's embrace and never leave.

She reached up and ran one finger lightly along the

line of his jaw, which was rough even though he had been shaven not two hours ago, when they had left Blythe House for the theater.

He murmured her name and moved his hands to her waist, pulling her even closer. Pressed against him, she marveled at the solidity of his chest. It was like leaning against a warm, breathing wall. Inhaling deeply, she filled her lungs with the deep, spicy scent of sandalwood and some other essence that she could not identify but likewise could not get enough of. A scent that belonged uniquely and irrevocably to this one person. The one person in all of London she could not have.

Abruptly, she leaned back, breaking the kiss. He released his hold on her waist, laying one arm gently on her elbow to keep her from stumbling.

"My deepest apologies, Cassandra." He gasped. "I should not—"

She reached up and laid a silencing finger across his lips, astonished at her boldness. A tingle ran up her spine as she remembered how the lips beneath her finger had explored her own lips just moments ago, calling up sensations she had not known herself capable of. "I should not have, either. But I cannot say I regret that I did."

He grinned, and she could see the spark of warm humor in his eyes even in the dim light of the stairwell. "Nor can I. Although I suppose I am no longer a paragon of propriety in your eyes?"

She laughed. "Kisses are only improper when they are not welcome. You did not notice any resistance on my part, did you?"

"Resistance seemed to be the last thing on either of our minds, if I may be so frank as to say so." The smile that she had so grown to adore over the last few weeks faded from his features. "But the fact remains that you were right to pull away. I am promised to another lady, and I will not break my word."

Cassandra sighed. "I know you won't. It is one of the reasons I . . . admire you so." To her shock, she realized she had almost said "love," censoring herself just in time.

Love? Could she really love the Earl of Winchfield? A man who was suspicious of wit, loathed London, and was more at home in a dusty barn than in a drawing room?

All of those things, she suddenly realized, were mere window dressing. What a man liked to do and where he liked to live were parts of his character, to be certain. But far more important was what a man *was*. And Ben, she knew, was a man of great value.

And yet he was determined to control everyone and everything who came across his path. If, by some amazing stroke of fortune, the earl found himself free of Lady Louisa, and if he then offered for Cassandra herself, could she possibly accept?

No.

The hypothetical situation was undeniably tempting. But reason compelled her to admit that a marriage between herself and the earl would be a disaster. It might be fun at first—the kiss they had just shared was proof enough of that. But what would happen as the years went on? Ben had already expressed dismay about her efforts to write plays. He would likely encourage her to cease them altogether if they had a family.

Whether she loved the earl or not—and she was not even sure that she wasn't simply addled by their kiss—she could not possibly tell him so. Such an admission would do neither of them any good.

"As I . . . *admire* you," said the earl, startling her. He was responding, of course, to her last statement. His emphasis on the verb gave her the uneasy feeling that he knew exactly what she had been about to say.

A strange silence settled over them. Lord Winchfield released her elbow, and she stepped away. Slowly, awareness of their situation returned to her.

"If we are to apprehend Mr. Dempster, we should probably make our way to the stairwell now," she said in a strained voice, even though she longed to stay precisely where she was.

"True." He smiled, but it was a sad expression. "If it turns out that Mr. Dempster cannot help me extract myself from my betrothal to Lady Louisa, then we should probably put what just happened out of our minds."

"Yes." And if it turned out that he *could* escape his promise to Lady Louisa, what then? The question hung unasked between them. A moment later, the silence of the theater was broken by a smattering of applause and cheers.

"The interval is beginning," she said, brushing past him and hurrying down the stairs. "Let us make haste, before we are swallowed by the crowd." Without glancing back, she descended the last few stairs and hurried across the lobby below. But even without looking, she could sense Ben on her heels. She had an uneasy feeling that, for the rest of her life, she would always know when he was near.

"There he is." Being tall had its advantages, Ben thought, as he easily spotted Mr. Dempster's bright hair in the throng of people spilling into the lobby from the stairs and the door leading into the main portion of the theater. "And we are in luck. Simpson is with him."

"Good." Behind him, Cassandra's voice was muted, as it had been ever since he had kissed her in the stairwell.

What had he been thinking, he wondered as he waited for Simpson and Dempster to approach them. Yes, Cassandra had looked so very tempting, with the dim light from a wall lantern shining on her blond curls. But he was not a man who gave in easily to every temptation. Doing so led only to disaster, in his experience.

There was no explaining impulsiveness, he told himself. He had acted like a wanton schoolboy, but it had been worth it. Every second.

No matter how hard he tried to focus on watching the two men make their way into the lobby, his mind remained fixed on the sensation of Cassandra in his arms. It was not that he had wide experience with women, but he had not spent the first thirty years of his life as a monk, either. And most of the women he had known had seemed like tiny china dolls in his embrace. He had been afraid of smothering them or breaking them, particularly because most of them had seemed so very still in his arms.

Cassandra had not been still. When she had arched upward and run her fingers through the hair at his nape, he had thought he would go mad. It had been all he could do to behave with even moderate restraint. He had not known just how ardently he had wanted to kiss her until he had held her and felt all his senses burst into flame. Everything about her had impinged on his consciousness with the force of a thunderstorm: her softness, her voice, her hair. A faint whisper of lavender scent still clung to his fingers.

It was ironic, really. At heart, he was just as much the barbarian as Lady Louisa had tried to paint him. He had not torn at Lady Cassandra's clothing, true, but he had had a very real desire to pick her up in his arms and carry her out of the theater, out of this benighted cesspool of London, and back to Dorsetshire, where in the privacy of his estate he could—

"Winchfield! It seems I can't go two steps in Town without stumbling over you."

Mercifully, Simpson had spotted him. Left to his own scattered devices, Ben would have missed his acquaintance's approach. Cassandra appeared equally distracted, as she had not given him any warning that the pair they awaited was coming towards them.

"Good evening, Simpson," he responded. "It's a pleasure to see you again."

Simpson looked toward the man beside him. "Dempster, may I introduce you to Benjamin Rowland, the Earl of Winchfield? Winchfield, this is an old school friend of mine, Bartholomew Dempster. He is recently returned from India."

Ben shook the shorter man's hand, relieved that he was indeed the man they sought. The question remained, however, whether he would have any interesting insight into Lady Louisa's behavior.

Turning to Cassandra, he introduced her to the two gentlemen. After they had exchanged pleasantries, Simpson asked, "Would you like to accompany us outside? It is devilish hot in here, and I would like to breathe some cooler air before returning to my seat."

The four of them emerged into the damp night air,

and Ben agreed with his friend that it was refreshing to escape the stuffy confines of the theater.

"I must admit that the air in the theater did not bother me at all. It is practically frosty, in comparison to the heat one endures in India." Dempster's voice was high and reedy, and he did have the lisp Lady Farnham had mentioned.

"That must have been a fascinating experience," said Cassandra. "What brings you back to London?"

"A few things. I enjoyed India, but I also longed to return home. There were some affairs here I wished to conclude."

Before Ben could press the man further on that topic, Dempster added, "I adore the theater, and there are so few opportunities to enjoy it in India. Seems like scant reason to travel halfway around the world, but I am in my element here."

"As am I," chimed in Cassandra. "Do you write plays as well as watch them?"

Ben suppressed an admiring smile. She wasted no time in trying to build bridges with their quarry.

"I have dabbled a bit," the blond man said with what Ben perceived as false modesty. It was clear that Dempster thought his writing efforts quite good.

"As do I!" Cassandra exclaimed. "In fact, I shall have a play produced in this very theater later this Season," she added in a bright voice.

She would? Ben had heard nothing of this. Surely she would have mentioned it to him? Perhaps it was just a ruse to capture Dempster's interest.

If it was, it worked. "Truly?" the man asked, leaning toward her. "How on earth did you manage that?"

"I submitted a few plays to a producer here, Mr.

Fisher. Perhaps I could arrange an introduction to him for you, if you like."

Dempster's eyes were as wide and avaricious as a cat's. "I would be most in your debt, Lady Cassandra."

"I would be happy to do so. Why don't you pay me a call tomorrow afternoon at, say, two o'clock? We could discuss it in more detail then."

"With pleasure, my lady."

She gave him the address of Blythe House. "That is one of the most prestigious streets in Mayfair!" he exclaimed.

"I am staying with my brother." Cassandra's voice revealed that she was nonplussed by the man's evident awe, as was Ben. Dempster's clothes were in the first stare of fashion, and he obviously employed an expensive tailor, judging by the cut. If he was the sort of person accustomed to such luxuries, he certainly should not have been unduly impressed by a Mayfair address.

"Did we not meet at Lady Farnham's masquerade the other night?" Ben asked. He wanted to be certain that they had the right gentleman.

Dempster squinted at him. "You do seem a bit familiar, my lord, and I *was* at the party. I think I may have seen you at a distance, but I do not believe we met."

Ben was wondering how he could delicately ask why Dempster had been seeking Lady Louisa at the party, when the gentleman saved him the trouble. "I was there mainly in the hopes of encountering an old friend. Are you acquainted with Lady Louisa Dennis?"

Ben breathed a sigh of relief. Dempster obviously had not heard about Ben's supposedly intimate acquaintance with Lady Louisa in the garden. He suspected that the blond man would soon be the last person in the *ton* to remain ignorant of it. "I know Lady Louisa, yes," he said carefully, schooling his features into what he hoped was a blank mask. "You say she is an old friend?"

"Oh, yes, we grew up together. I have been trying to meet with her ever since I returned to London, but she is never at home and has not responded to the cards I have left at her house."

"I believe she has a most active social life. I'm sure she will return your calls eventually." Ben's mind was only half on his words. Lady Louisa was avoiding Dempster, just as they had suspected. But why?

"I certainly hope so, as I have news that I know shall interest her greatly." He beamed, a self-satisfied smile that only confirmed Ben's sense of the man's boundless self-confidence.

"If I see her before you do, would you like me to relay a message?" Cassandra piped up.

He turned to her. "Thank you, my lady, but no. 'Tis a bit of a private matter between myself and Lady Louisa, and I would like to tell her in person, if it can be managed."

"Oh, I am certain it can be managed," Cassandra said with an odd little smile. Ben could almost read her mind. He suspected that there might be another guest at Blythe House when Mr. Dempster arrived tomorrow afternoon.

"It was so very kind of you to invite me to visit, Lady Elinor," Lady Louisa burbled as she rattled her spoon inside her teacup, setting Cassandra's teeth on edge. "I was concerned that, given the . . . unconventional nature of my betrothal to your brother, you would bear me ill will."

"Nonsense," Elinor replied with a bright smile. Ellie really should be on the stage, Cassandra thought, hoping that she was concealing her own contempt for their guest half as well as Ellie was. "As we are soon to be sisters, I wanted to take this opportunity to get to know you a little better. Would you like some more cake?"

"I do believe I would," Lady Louisa said, selecting two plump pieces of lemon cake from the tray Elinor proffered. "Your chef is most skilled. I hope that dear Lord Winchfield and I shall be able to hire staff half as able when we are wed."

"*Dear*" indeed, Cassandra thought, sneaking a covert glance at the earl. He was coiled as tightly as a snake about to spring and did not look at all impressed by Lady Louisa's endearment. If he was so dear, it was remarkable that Lady Louisa did not feel comfortable using his Christian name.

Cassandra thought of the last time she had spoken Ben's name aloud and felt a slow tingle that started in her toes and shimmered up her body until even the ends of her hair seemed to spark. What a decidedly odd position to be in, she reflected—to be chatting with Ben's fiancée, with whom he had not shared so much as a kiss, while reveling in the knowledge of just what being kissed by the Earl of Winchfield was like. What a strange, strange Season this was turning out to be.

A scratch sounded at the door. A moment later, the Blythes' butler entered the room. "Lady Cassandra, you have a visitor."

She gave silent thanks that the servant had

remembered her instructions not to announce the name of her guest. "Thank you, Cannings. Please show him—or her—upstairs."

If Lady Louisa found this breach of protocol odd, she did not mention it. She was probably loath to criticize anything about the family she had managed to trick her way into, for fear of causing any kind of rift before the vows were official.

Lady Louisa launched into a story about someone she had met in Oxford Street that morning, but Cassandra barely followed a word. Almost all of her attention was focused on listening to someone coming up the stairs. He had reached the top; she could hear muffled steps on the deep carpet in the corridor. The door opened.

"Lady Cassandra!" said Bartholomew Dempster as he spotted her from the doorway. She rose, as etiquette demanded, but she kept her gaze fastened firmly on Lady Louisa. The red-haired woman dropped her plate of cake to a small table with a clatter.

"Barthy," she whispered.

Mr. Dempster, likely attracted by the noise of the crashing dish more than by Lady Louisa's barely audible reaction, turned toward her. He stopped. Froze. "Louisa!"

Well, Cassandra's hunch had been correct on one score: Lady Louisa and the mysterious Mr. Dempster did know each other well. But the bluestocking was not reacting at all in the way Cassandra had suspected she might. She was shocked, without doubt. But instead of fleeing the room, she was looking at Mr. Dempster rather as a hungry horse might eye a manger of hay. She scrambled to her feet.

Cassandra glanced at Ben, but his eyebrows were

knotted below a furrowed forehead. Evidently, he was as bemused as she by the scene unfolding before them.

By the time Cassandra returned her attention to their visitors, Mr. Dempster had crossed the room. "Louisa. I thought I would never find you." To Cassandra's utter astonishment, the blond man gathered Lady Louisa into a crushing embrace, and the object of his affection did not resist.

"I've been in Chelsea all this time," Cassandra heard Lady Louisa murmur.

"I know. I've tried to see you. Every day."

"Frederick wouldn't permit it. I begged, but he was adamant. He has even been watching my correspondence. He destroyed at least two letters I tried to send you in care of the Expedition Club."

"I believe you. I even ran him to ground at a gaming hell on Pall Mall, but he disappeared through the back entrance before I could speak to him."

Over by the fireplace, Ben cleared his throat. With a collective jump, as though they had completely forgotten there was anyone else in the room, Mr. Dempster and Lady Louisa detached themselves from each other and turned to face him. Mr. Dempster had a slightly shamefaced expression, but Lady Louisa's eyes were wide and her skin was ashen.

"Forgive my curiosity, but how exactly are you acquainted with Mr. Dempster, Lady Louisa?" Ben asked.

When the red-haired woman did not answer immediately, Mr. Dempster spoke up. "She's a bit shy, but I'm not ashamed to shout it from the rooftops. Lady Louisa is my fiancée."

CHAPTER FOURTEEN

In the wake of Dempster's startling announcement, a number of things happened at once.

Lady Louisa launched into an incoherent explanation of the situation that Ben could barely follow.

Ellie started to laugh with what seemed to be relief, tears streaming down her face.

Richard, who until this point had remained silent in a small chair by the fireplace, strolled across the room and clapped Ben soundly on the back.

Dempster looked wildly around the room, evidently trying to determine why his statement had caused such an uproar.

And Cassandra—well, Cassandra looked as though someone had given her the keys to Rundell and Bridge, along with *carte blanche* to select any item she fancied from the vitrines of the famous jeweler. Her smile could have illuminated Pall Mall brighter than any gaslight.

As for Ben himself, he was still absorbing the extraordinary news. Dempster's news, if it was true, would release Ben completely from Lady Louisa and her schemes. Proof of a previous commitment to another was one of the very few ironclad reasons one could have for breaking a betrothal without recrimination.

Ben's heart pounded as he realized just how much worse this situation could have been. What if he had been able to procure the special license, only to be standing up in front of half the *ton* with Lady Louisa at St. George's when Mr. Dempster pressed his claim from the congregation? A claim such as Dempster's was precisely the reason the Church of England wedding service included a line that asked parishioners to declare any reason that might prevent the couple from marrying.

As the full import of what could have happened dawned on him, a cold, implacable fury swept through Ben. He clenched his hands into fists as he turned to Lady Louisa and cut her off in midsentence.

"Did you ever once stop to think, Lady Louisa, how your trickery could have exposed me—us—to even greater shame and ridicule than we currently face?" With extreme effort, he kept his voice low and modulated, when what he wanted to do was shout until he was hoarse. "What if Mr. Dempster had raised his voice in protest during our wedding? Can you think of the scandal that would have engendered? Do you realize I would have been branded a wife-stealer throughout the length and breadth of England?" At the thought, he felt his whole body stiffen. This foolish chit might have damaged his reputation, and his hopes of making a good match, beyond repair.

"Wedding? Wife-stealer? Louisa, what in the name of heaven is Lord Winchfield talking about?" Dempster's face showed nothing but utter confusion. The poor man appeared to be just as much a pawn in this affair as Ben.

Lady Louisa returned to the settee and collapsed onto it before slowly turning her attention to Dempster. Her face was scarlet. "It was all Frederick's idea. He bullied me into it. He'd been agitating for months for me to make a rich match this Season, but your letter detailing your plans to return to England tipped the scales. Frederick told me I had to marry a rich man before you arrived back in London. Before you could thwart the plan. When he heard you were here, he increased the pressure, and forbade me to see you."

"But why, Louisa? Did your feelings change?" Dempster's voice was soft.

Lady Louisa shook her head. A long strand of red hair came loose and fell into her eyes. She suddenly looked as miserable and vulnerable as a lost child, and Ben felt a reluctant glimmer of sympathy for her.

"No. I do not love Lord Winchfield, and my feelings for you are as constant as ever, Bartholomew. I have wanted to marry you since the moment we met at the fair in Billington."

He smiled. "You were a very perceptive twelve-year-old, to see past my poverty at that time." But then his smile faded. "If your feelings remained constant, why did you give in to Frederick's badgering?"

"You don't know what it's been like," Lady Louisa said with a weary sigh. "Frederick has been adamant that I could not marry you because you had such a modest income. When I told him I would run away rather than submit to his demands, he—well, he convinced me not to." Her voice was laced with unmistakable revulsion. She paused, as if she would say more about the means Halmond had employed, but then decided better of it.

Ben felt another surge of anger at the viscount, but

he could not ask Louisa to lay out her private shame for the delectation of near strangers just so that Ben could determine how, exactly, Halmond had coerced his sister to obey him.

After a moment, Louisa spoke again. "I was too ashamed to write this in a letter, but Frederick lost our house in an ill-conceived wager at Boodles last year."

Dempster sucked in his breath. "It wasn't entailed?"

"No, oddly. Our ancestors had a very cavalier attitude toward legal matters." She looked away for a moment, then returned her attention to Dempster. "We have survived on the kindness of relations in the interim, moving from home to home, never staying anywhere long enough to become a burden. We used almost the last of Frederick's inheritance to lease and staff the house in Chelsea for the Season."

"If Frederick is so desperate to bring a fortune into the family, why didn't he marry one himself?" Dempster's voice was harsh with loathing.

Lady Louisa's hands fluttered in her lap. "He tried. In fact, until a month ago, it looked fairly certain that he would marry a rich Cit's daughter. Her father runs a drapery shop and was avid to see his daughter marry into the peerage. But then she met Lord Alsonby at a horse race in Hampshire, and they immediately became smitten with each other. Alsonby has plenty of blunt and several estates. The father, naturally enough, decided that that would be a more propitious match. Frederick was livid. And by that point, of course, our financial situation and Frederick's gambling habits had become well known, and most of the ladies of the *ton* would have nothing to do with him." She sighed again. "No, if anyone was to rescue us from this situation, it had to be me."

Ben stifled an impulse to speak out against Halmond. What sort of man could expose his own sister to such misery, all because he hadn't had the sense to walk away from a card table? It defied belief. But he held his tongue, as he wanted to hear the rest of this extraordinary tale.

"I blame myself in part for this tangle," Dempster said.

"You?" chimed in Cassandra, echoing the question in Ben's mind. "How are you in any way at fault?"

The blond man looked at her. "My foolish pride has caused me to withhold some information from Louisa that might well have spared us all from Halmond's machinations. You see, I have had the great good luck to make my fortune in India."

"Your fortune?" Lady Louisa's eyes were wide.

Dempster nodded. He knelt down beside Louisa's chair and took her hands into his. "I made some profitable investments in India. Some industrial schemes and several farms. Tea. Spices. I will tell you all about it later. But the fact is, I am not the indigent squire you knew back in Billington. Not to be boastful, but I am a very wealthy man, Louisa. I wanted to see your face when I told you the news, so I refrained from mentioning anything of my good luck in my letters. I wanted to surprise you." He sighed. "What a foolish mistake."

"But all is not lost," Cassandra said, crossing the room and taking a seat next to Louisa on the settee. "Even though a number of people know of Lady Louisa's betrothal to Lord Winchfield, your prior claim to Lady Louisa's hand would take precedence in a court of law, should it come to that—which it won't," she hastened to add in response to the horrified expression on Dempster's face.

The blond man's attachment to Louisa was obvious. He would not relinquish his claim to her. As a result, Louisa would be married and safe from most of the scandal that might otherwise ensue. Halmond would get his money and thus leave his sister in peace. Ben truly was free of the lot of them.

Relief washed through him in great, sweeping waves. He leaned heavily against the back of the chair as the tension drained from his muscles.

He had been spared, but the solution had not been his. From beginning to end, the road that had led them to Dempster had been paved by Cassandra. And if he had known what she was doing, he would have tried to put a stop to it. As usual, his attempts to control a situation would have simply led him closer to disaster.

"Do you have proof of your betrothal?" Cassandra asked Dempster.

"Everyone in our parish in Billington would know of it. The banns were read before I left for India."

She nodded. "That should be more than sufficient. And as it stands, your wealth should allay Lord Halmond's concerns—although, were I you, I would do my best to ensure that he is not able to gain access to one penny of it."

Dempster grinned. "You are a mind reader, Lady Cassandra. Of course, I will not see my new brother-in-law destitute. But if he desires a roof over his head, he shall have to come and live with us. I will not bankroll him to buy another house he can gamble away." He stood and held out his hand to Lady Louisa, who rose as well.

"I hope you will forgive me, Lady Cassandra, if I postpone our conversation about the theater world until another time," Dempster said as the couple began to move toward the door. "Louisa and I have much to discuss."

"Of course," Cassandra murmured.

Louisa suddenly stopped, whispered something to her fiancé, and returned to stand beside Ben's chair.

"I am so sorry that I involved you in Frederick's wretched scheme," she said in a low voice. To her credit, she looked him right in the eye. "Georgina assured me that you were an honorable gentleman, so I knew there was a good chance that you would agree to marry me once I engineered the scene at the masquerade."

Dempster looked as though he very much wanted to know what that scene had involved, but Ben did not enlighten him. Louisa, no doubt, would apprise Dempster of the details later. Ben's thoughts returned to one word Louisa had just said in her apology. *Georgina*. Would the demmed woman haunt him to the end of his days?

"But it is because you are such an honorable gentleman that I feel particularly ashamed of my role in this affair. Please accept my most abject apologies, Lord Winchfield."

"With pleasure, Lady Louisa. And do not judge yourself too harshly. It is not an easy life, I suspect, to be an impoverished sister subject to her brother's whims. I hold Lord Halmond far more to blame in this situation than I do you." The absence of rancor he now felt toward Louisa surprised him. Halmond would do well not to find himself alone in a deserted lane with Ben, but Louisa had been very ill used, and he could not carry a grudge against her for acting as she had. Obviously, she had been concerned with self-preservation.

Louisa smiled. "Thank you. That is very kind." She looked down at the carpet for a brief moment, then raised her gaze to his once more. "If it would make things easier for you, I shall let the reason for our betrothal—and its end—become widely known in the *ton*."

"As to the first, I'm afraid I may have already put those wheels in motion," Cassandra said, her voice sheepish. "I told Lady Farnham that you had created a false scandal at the masquerade. I'm sorry, Lady Louisa, but news of the scheme has probably traveled halfway around Mayfair by now. You know how Lady Farnham likes to talk."

"I do, indeed," Lady Louisa said with a slight smile. "But do not feel bad, Lady Cassandra. I opened myself up to scandalous talk when I chose to give in to Frederick's bullying, so I must pay the price."

Ben's slight kernel of admiration for Lady Louisa grew. She had behaved badly, but at least she was willing to take responsibility for her actions.

"The talk shall not bother me unduly, in any case. If Bartholomew agrees, we shall soon be wed, and I shan't care what anyone says about me then."

"We shall be wed as soon as we can obtain a license!" Dempster's voice was gleeful, and Ben felt a slight stab of envy for the other man's happiness.

"Don't hold out great hopes for the Archbishop of Canterbury," he said. "They're being demmed stingy with special licenses these days."

"Oh, I think I'd rather return to Billington and be married in the village church. What do you think, my dear?"

"I agree wholeheartedly. The sooner I am shot of London, the better." Lady Louisa laid her hand on

Dempster's arm. "If you will excuse us, I believe we will take our leave. I cannot thank you enough for arranging things so that Mr. Dempster and I could finally meet each other face-to-face."

With that, the couple said their farewells and departed, doubtless to discuss many things. When the door closed behind them, a stunned silence settled on the Blythe House drawing room.

"Whatever I expected from this afternoon's meeting, I certainly did not expect *that*," Cassandra said finally.

"I agree, although I cannot say I am sorry that things turned out as they did." Ben grinned. Now that Louisa and her fiancé had departed, he felt curiously energized.

Elinor stood and gave her husband a speaking look. "I am so glad you have been released from your betrothal to Lady Louisa," she said, crossing the room and giving Ben a quick hug. "It has been a harrowing few days," she added as she straightened, "and I am in need of some rest. And I believe Richard has some affairs he wanted to attend to this afternoon. Didn't you, Richard?"

"Yes, yes, of course," Blythe said, shooting to his feet. "Must be off. Things to do. Congratulations, Winchfield." Once again, his brother-in-law clapped him awkwardly on the shoulder. "And good thinking, Cassandra. If you hadn't thought to interrogate Lady Farnham, Lady Louisa's promise to Dempster might never have come to light."

Within moments, the Blythes had departed, leaving Ben alone with Cassandra. As he had often had cause to do as a child, Ben blessed his sister for her perception and tact. He desperately wanted to speak to Lady

Cassandra in private, but what he would say to her, he did not know.

As it turned out, Cassandra spoke first. "I am so happy for you," she said, her warm voice like balm on his frayed nerves.

"As your brother said, my happiness can be laid directly at your door. I am forever in your debt."

Her eyes sparkled. "I shall have to determine just how I shall collect that marker."

He blinked. Was she implying what he suspected she was implying? Remembering the kiss they had shared in the stairwell at the theater, he felt his mouth go dry.

The theatre. He suddenly recalled a question he'd been meaning to ask since the previous evening, but had forgotten in the maelstrom of activity surrounding Dempster's visit. "Have your really submitted your plays to a theater producer?"

Her smile faded. "Yes. That was not simply a ruse to entice Mr. Dempster into our trap. Mr. Fisher has offered to buy one of my older plays. He is also very interested in *The Gentleman's Dilemma,* the script I'm revising now." With a sigh, she stood and walked toward the window. As always, he admired the easy grace with which she moved.

"Why didn't you tell me?" A month ago, even a week ago, he would not have thought the sale of a play would be anything to aspire to. But knowing how much it mattered to Cassandra, he wanted to shout with excitement at her news.

Her back remained to him as she pulled aside the heavy velvet drape and stared out at the square below. "I did not think you would approve."

Her words, pronounced in a flat voice, cut him to

the quick. *Approve?* As though she were a wayward child, and her dreams were unworthy of recognition?

Of course she would think that. With chagrin, he remembered the comments he had made at the picnic. He had been so scathing in his dismissal of the theater—a world he didn't even understand. Ironically, it had been a night at the theater that had been his salvation.

More to the point, it had been Cassandra who had been his salvation. When events had spiraled far past his ability to control them, she had stepped in with intuition and intelligence to rescue him from the morass.

And yet she thought she needed his *approval?* It was beyond comprehension.

Suddenly, he knew what he had to do.

It was entirely possible that Cassandra would laugh him out of the room. It was ludicrous, really, to suppose that she would accept an offer from him after turning down proposals from half the *ton*.

If he spoke up and she scoffed at him, he would go back to Dorsetshire heartbroken. But at least he wouldn't return home a coward. For once in his life, it was time to take a risk whose outcome he could not predict.

Slowly, deliberately, he stood and crossed the room.

Cassandra sensed Ben's approach before she even heard his footfalls on the carpet. Something in the air in the room behind her had changed. She didn't dare turn around for fear of altering the strange silence that had settled around them. It reminded her of the cocoon that had wrapped itself around the two of them on the riverside at Richmond, after he had pulled Alice from the water.

She shivered slightly as she remembered that day. It had been the first day she'd realized just how different Benjamin Rowland was from the *bon vivants* of the *ton*.

So different was he, unfortunately, that he was obviously appalled by the news of her play's success. He had not said a word since she'd explained the reason for her reticence. It was clear she had been right not to tell him of her good fortune.

A carriage clopped by in the street below. In the distance, a flower girl's cries echoed down a side street. Cassandra resolutely kept her focus on the world beyond this room, until she felt the earl's warm breath on her hair.

"Approve?" he whispered, so softly she almost didn't hear him. "I approve most heartily of everything you do, my lady."

Her heart slammed into her rib cage at his words, and threatened to burst altogether when his large hands came to rest on her waist. Every bone and sinew and muscle in her body urged her to turn around and relinquish herself to his embrace. But something held her back, made her anxious to keep him at a distance.

"You were right," she murmured, desperate to say anything, to fill the air with words. If she didn't, she would surely fall into his embrace, and that would be most unwise. "About wit."

"About *wit?*" His low voice was close to her ear.

"I was wrong," she said, refusing to meet his eyes. "Before I met you, I made great sport out of people like Louisa Dennis. And until the true facts of her life came to light just now, I could not seem to think anything but ill of her. I should have taken a page from your book and been less critical."

"I'm not a saint, Cassandra. I had quite a few unkind thoughts about Lady Louisa myself. And I'm having a few very unsaintly thoughts at the minute."

With the slightest pressure of his hands, he coaxed her to turn around. When she did, his face was just inches from hers. She remembered how his cheek, and his lips, had felt under her fingertips.

"I don't wish to speak of Lady Louisa," he went on. "Cassandra, I want—" He stopped.

"Yes?" A mixture of dread and anticipation flooded her mind, almost washing away all conscious thought and leaving nothing but emotion and sensation.

He gripped her waist. "I want you to know that—I'm not averse to spending the Season in London. Every year."

Her breath caught in her throat. "But what about your studies? You shouldn't give those up."

"I could foster an ant colony in a Mayfair stable yard just as well as in my barn in Dorsetshire. Besides, a scientist named Charles Goodale is forming a new society of scientific scholars that will meet here in London during the Season. It will be an unparalleled opportunity to increase my scientific knowledge." He drew her toward him. "But even if I had to spend every day of the Season doing nothing but attending balls and routs and masquerades, I would do it gladly, if it meant I could be here with you."

Exultation slowly built within her. It hadn't been her fear of leaving London that had made her reluctant to give in to her feelings for Ben. It had been her fear that he would give up his dreams for *her*. "And I would spend every day of the year in the country, if I could spend them with you." She would, she knew with a certainty she had rarely felt about anything.

"What about your plays?" His brow wrinkled in a most endearing way.

"Certainly, it would is useful to be in Town once in a while, to consult with Mr. Fisher. But if you can set up an ant colony in Mayfair, I could certainly set up a study . . . anywhere." It seemed to be tempting fate to say any more.

"Could you? Even in Dorsetshire?"

She nodded. "Even in Dorsetshire."

"For the second time in a week, I believe I'm about to make an offer to a lady. But this time, I mean it." He drew her into his arms. "Marry me, Cassandra. Please. My life won't be the same without you."

The simplicity of his words undid her. No flowery phrases, no poetic declarations. Just honest truth. Just what she'd been looking for all along, if she'd only known.

"Yes, Ben," she said as she stretched up on tiptoe to kiss him. "I would be honored to be your wife."

More Regency Romance
From Zebra